9/17/14

Betty,

Hope you enjoy the

journey!

Love,
Marilyn
Grif andn

PS— love seeing your
reunion pics - looks
like fun!

Marra Dallas

Marilyn Timpanaro

"No man is an island, entire of itself."

John Donne

Marra Dallas

by

Marilyn Timpanaro

ISBN 9781492972174

Printed in the USA

To my precious family ~

Ron, Ronnie & Jessica, Kristen & Steve, Jake & Jenna

Your love and devotion gives me hope for the future

To Mae ~ my inspiration

To Sadie, Jake Dog & Ivy, and Labrador Retrievers everywhere ~ the epitome of loyalty and affection

Marilyn Timpanaro

PART I

1969, Age 15

The Incident

Death changes everything. I kept trying to focus on sights and sounds in order to keep my thoughts at bay, but it was becoming an exercise in futility. I could feel the blood, warm and sticky on my hands, and I could see the pulsing red strobe intermittently lighting the night, sporadically illuminating the shadowed grate in front of me. The car smelled of cigarettes, fried food, and something funkier - I didn't even want to imagine what it might be. The static of voices squawked from the radio unintelligibly, and the noises outside were muffled through closed windows.

A man hollered, "Sir, step back, sir!"

The car shook as fists pounded its hood, demanding vengeance.

"You little bitch! I'll fucking kill you! You're dead, do you hear me? Dead!"

There were sounds of a scuffle and raised voices as I shut my eyes tightly, determined not to look. I'd seen too much this day, and I couldn't bear anymore. Besides, I already knew it was Phil Marcucci, Rocco's brother. Too bad he hadn't shown up *before* the cops did, so that I could have killed him, too. The family could have had a two-fer, stick them both in the same box and close the lid!

I was surprised that the cops were holding him back because, as my daddy used to say, they were all in Marcucci's pocket. Phil owned this shithole of a town and most of the locals were related to him in some way, cousins, in-laws, or illegitimate sons and daughters. Most of those who weren't relatives were on his payroll because Phil owned a restaurant, gas station, pizza joint, a couple of bars, and a construction company. Most of the cops in town were moonlighting for him, or somebody in *their* family worked for *his* Family, that's family with a capital F.

I think that they might have let him kill me if they hadn't already had me locked in the back seat of the cruiser. They could have said that they couldn't stop him - it all happened too fast, and then he would have claimed self-defense. But there were too many witnesses now. The neighbors were out in their nightclothes, huddled in small circles around the perimeter of the property, pointing and whispering over the most excitement they'd had since my old man crashed his pickup into the dead-end wall, drunk as a skunk, precipitating his early retirement from the Oaklawn, New Jersey police force.

CHAPTER ONE

Daddy's 'accident' was five years before 'the incident', just days before Mama threw his sorry ass out for good. My brother Will got out of Dodge, joining the Air Force right after that fiasco, leaving my sister Shelby and me to face the music alone. Mama, who'd always had a flair for the dramatic, refused to show her pretty face in public after what she called Daddy's *"beastial display of barbarianism"*, in her finest Southern drawl. Mama's self-imposed exile forced Shelby and me to become her unwitting slaves.

Every day after school Mama would have our list waiting - groceries from the Grand Union, beauty supplies from Walgreens, or perhaps a new pink cardigan from Lobel's Department Store. Being only ten years old at the time, I felt privileged to be trusted with cash and responsibility. I'd sing all the way to the stores and then back again, just so I didn't have to listen to Shelby's whining and complaining. That first summer I had memorized all of the lyrics to my new Beatles' *Rubber Soul* album, and drove Shelby to distraction by singing my favorites at the top of my lungs.

Shelby had just turned thirteen and was mortified by the entire affair. She didn't want to be seen grocery shopping either, especially with her bratty little sister in tow. She'd sulk and complain the entire time, leaving me stuck to do all of the shopping by myself. Except, of course, if there was something Shelby wanted, then she was only too happy to peruse the racks and aisles. It was seldom, though, that Mama had enough money for us to buy something for ourselves. Shelby was outraged, believing that she deserved the very same nice, new things that her wealthier classmates had. Every single day upon returning home she'd threaten to run away, to which Mama would respond sweetly, "Then why don't you just pack up your bags and go on now, Shelby dahlin', before you forget all about it?"

Invariably, Shelby would scowl and go to her room, slamming the door behind her. Of course, that meant that I had the pleasure of putting all of the groceries that I'd shopped for by myself, away by myself. Mama would never have dreamed of hauling Shelby out of her room and make her help me, because Mama didn't want to have to deal with Shelby's sulky attitude. Mama knew that I was irritated that, once again, I was stuck doing all of the work alone. She would coo words of encouragement as I toiled with bottles and cans, lining them up like soldiers on parade.

"My goodness, Miss Marra! You show 'nuff are a pro-fessional marke-tee-ah! Why darlin', you could have your own grocery store! You'd put that Grand Union outta business in no time. The ladies would be so impressed with your neat and tidy store, they'd never set foot in that big ol' messy store again!"

I knew she was bullshitting me, but I liked it all the same. After all, a compliment *is* a compliment. Shelby was the pretty one, the one Mama was always fawning over: "You're so beautiful, Shelby, please don't scowl like that darlin', you're gonna get wrinkles on your pretty face!" or "Shelby darlin', your hair is shinin' so bright, just like the Sun himself kissed your beautiful head!"

I was the plain one, so Mama had to reach into her bag of tricks to find ways to build me up. I was organized, punctual, and a straight-A student, but I would rather have been pretty, instead. Shelby's straight, blonde, shiny hair looked like that of all of the models in the fashion magazines, while my brown curls were a tangled mess. Shelby's golden-hazel eyes were almond-shaped, and they turned up on the ends, which gave them the appearance of a smile, even when she was in a foul mood. They were probably just happy to be set over those high cheekbones, tiny nose, and bow-shaped, pink mouth. My eyes were like big, green marbles, round and boring. Shelby was taller than me, and she was more narrow than I was, so I'd never fit properly in any of her beautifully coordinated outfits. I always thought that if I looked like Shelby I'd be happy, but she never seemed to be. She'd always say, "I hate this house and everything in it!", and I'd wondered if she'd meant me too, but I was always too scared to ask her. I'd spend hours thinking up ways to please her, but I was never successful. Shelby was un-please-able.

Shelby was older than me, prettier than me, and way more popular than I was. I had one friend, Jayne, while Shelby had dozens. Shelby and her pals went everywhere together like a pack of jackals. They'd talk and laugh until I got within earshot, and then Shelby would give them 'the look', and they'd all stop talking about whatever it was that was so funny and wait for me to leave. They all called me 'Shelby's little sister', never Marra. Shelby was the ringleader, that was for sure. One or two of her friends were kind to me whenever Shelby wasn't around, but as soon as she'd show up, they'd turn frosty.

I didn't mind running Mama's errands all the time, but what I *did* mind was the way Shelby took it out on me, like it was *my* fault that she was stuck doing menial things that interfered with her social life. She might have thought that it was my fault for not being mature enough to go alone, and I would have, but Mama would not allow it.

Life went on that way for three years until Mama met Rocco Marcucci at 'Back to School' night. He was there with his daughter Susanne, who was in Shelby's Italian class. Shelby just *had* to take Italian because Greg Varino was taking Italian, and she'd spent the last school year stalking him. I believe that she would've signed up for varsity football in order to be close to him if they'd let her. At least Greg had a valid reason for taking Italian class, his grandma was *off the boat* and spoke no English. Shelby, on the other hand, never did anything for anyone unless she was forced to. The book cover of her Italian text was decorated with the initials *GV* surrounded by hearts, subtlety not being one of Shelby's strong suits.

Marcucci showed up at our house the next day with a box of chocolates and a dozen long-stemmed, red roses. Mama had practically drooled all over him the night before in Mr. Abramo's classroom, encouraging this visit. I thought Marcucci was a dork, with his slicked-back hair, sharkskin suit, and burgundy tie with the dollar-sign tie clip. Mama thought he was handsome and charming, and when he appeared at our front door, her southern accent seemed to escalate full-tilt.

"Why Mista Mahcoo-chi, Ah do declay-ah!" she'd said, while batting her big, green, doe eyes at him like some silly, southern belle.

Mama had sprayed Avon's Scent of the Month, *Unforgettable*, around the house to cover the wet-dog smell left by Benny the Stink, our English Springer-mutt mix, and I was choking on it. I had just turned thirteen and believed that my mother was the most embarrassing woman on the planet. I was sure that in all of New Jersey there was not another mother with a southern accent who wore low-cut, frilly dresses. The fact that she was mine was a curse that was visited upon me by some mean and vengeful god. When she sipped on her cooking sherry or some cheap Chianti that came in a wicker-covered bottle, her accent deepened, sickening me to my very core. But this slick *"Eye-talian"*, as Mama called him, seemed to eat it up. She extended her hand to him, palm down, and he brought it up to his lips and kissed it gently, causing her to swoon.

"Oh, mah heavens! A real gentleman callah, that's what ya'll ah!"

I just couldn't take another second of it, and ran up the stairs, two at a time, to call Jayne on my pink princess phone. I needed to express my disgust and embarrassment appropriately. Jayne did little to comfort my dismay, because she thought my mother was glamorous and exciting, "like someone out of a Tennessee Williams play", to which I'd respond, "I've always hated Tennessee Williams."

Jayne's mother, on the other hand, was truly wonderful. Edith Lansing Mitchell was tall and willowy, with platinum hair and tasteful makeup. She shopped 'uptown' for designer clothing that looked 'smart'. Her accent was Eastern aristocratic, nasal, and low. She had a Patrician nose and large, ice-blue eyes. Her home looked like something out of Good Housekeeping. Edith called her curtains 'window treatments', and her walls had wood at the top, as well as at the bottom – it was something she called 'crown molding', and I thought that was appropriate for someone as regal as she.

Edith was engaged to Charlie, a publisher whose office was in Manhattan. She'd meet with him in the city for luncheons between her shopping sprees at Saks Fifth Avenue, Bloomingdale's, and wherever else she might fancy. Edith and Charlie would often take Jayne to the early show at The Improv comedy club, and then to a late dinner at P.J. Clarke's on Third Avenue. Every famous person they'd encounter seemed to be Charlie's best friend, including Ed Sullivan. Every so often they'd invite me to come along, and I'd pretend to be their other daughter, secretly wishing it were true. Jayne believed that her mother and Charlie were typical and boring, while my mother and Rocco were exotic and exciting. I would have given my left arm in a trade.

CHAPTER TWO

My mother was entranced by Rocco Marcucci, and after he'd left that first night, she danced around the kitchen singing *Just In Time*. Shelby and I rolled our eyes at one another and criticized him to Mama, but she wouldn't hear of it, she thought Rocco was dreamy. It went on that way for a full year and a half, as Rocco wined and dined Mama, and impressed her with his diamond pinkie ring, and gold Cadillac. Mama would go on and on about how you could tell a classy man by the car he drove and the jewelry he wore, but I'd seen class in Edith's boyfriend Charlie, and he wore no ostentatious jewelry, and drove a rather plain, black Buick. I would have loved to share that insight with Mama, but I knew she'd take it as a personal affront to her intelligence. Mama, as Daddy used to say, wasn't the sharpest knife in the drawer. As it turned out, those were very prophetic words.

Marcucci would take Mama to dinner at his brother Phil's restaurant, *La Dolce Vita*, near the river. The eatery sported a miniature Trevi fountain outside, into which we were required to throw coins at every visit. Each time Mama would say, "Now y'all don't forget to make that special wish!" and I'd think to myself, *I wish we weren't here!* Inside, the restaurant was a series of darkened rooms that sported gaudy, gold-flocked wallpaper and ornate candelabras that dripped with faux diamonds. Mama thought it was classy, but I thought it was tacky. When Shelby and I were required to come along, Mama would force us to wear our Sunday dresses with hose and heels. We'd try to get our hair looking decent, so Mama wouldn't chase us around the kitchen with the curling iron that she'd heated on the gas stove, inevitably leaving ugly, red welts on our necks.

While other mothers were forbidding their teenage daughters from wearing makeup in 1967, my mother insisted upon it. We had to curl our lashes, and pucker our lips for Mama's latest shades from Avon. No eye shadow was deemed 'too blue' for Mizz Charlotte Eveann Delores Whitford Dunne. Behind her back, Shelby called her 'Charlotte the Harlot', and would make me swear under threat of death never to repeat that to anyone. As I was always trying to win Shelby's approval, I never would have dreamed of crossing her.

Jayne had gotten her hair cut like Twiggy's, the most chic style of the day; but Mama forbade my sister and me to have short hair. Shoulder-length was the minimum, and for me that meant when my hair was *not* wet, because when it dried, it curled up shorter. I would have loved to have had one of those short Twiggy-cuts, but I knew better than to argue. Mama always said that the rule of thumb for a real lady was 'tresses and dresses', and that meant long hair and long skirts – well, long for the style of the time. Jayne got to wear mini-skirts, but we knew better than to try and pass that by Mama, who'd have us stand up straight while she'd measure from the center of our knees to the hem of our skirts with a ruler. Two inches was the maximum allowed under Charlotte's Law, and that was pushing it. She preferred that the hem 'skim' our knees, but thankfully, Shelby had thrown such a fit over it, that Mama amended it to the Two-Inch-Rule. Shelby, being older and so much wiser than I, always chose skirts over dresses so she could hike them up once she was out of Mama's field of vision. It took me years to catch on to her little trick, but by then I was already stuck with owning mostly dresses.

Our hair and wardrobe was the least of our worries after Mama took up with Rocco Marcucci. Shelby and I quickly came to hate him, not only because of who he was, but because of who my mother would become while in his presence. He had Mama wrapped around his pinkie, ring and all, and she'd dote on him like he was the second coming of Christ on a shortcake. Mama thought it was *'international'* when he'd speak *'Eye-talian'* with his goombahs at the restaurant. I thought he was rude. Mama would sit there gazing at him, not understanding a single word he was saying (and, might I add, neither did Shelby - for all the good her Italian class did her) like he was reciting poetry.

Why Mama had chosen this slime ball to replace Daddy was a *puzzlement*, to use one of her own words. Had it been up to us, we would have paired her with Judge Delacroix, whose late wife had been our piano teacher. We knew that Mama thought he was handsome, because she'd always comment that the Judge favored Gregory Peck, whom she'd called *'a fine specimen of manhood'*.

The Judge was retired and quite a bit older than Mama, but we knew he was in love with her – even before Mrs. D passed away. His first name was Jacques, but he was all-American, as his family had settled in New Jersey in the 1600s. The Judge and his wife had never had any children of their own, but they owned about a dozen cats that had their own bedroom, and an outdoor playhouse. Shelby and I called it the *cathouse*, and that drove Mama insane. She'd tell us not to use such profanity in her house, and we'd look at each other like she'd fallen off the deep end, us not realizing what the connotation was.

The Judge played the piano even better than Mrs. D, who was the piano teacher. Mrs. D, who always used sheet music, played in a stilted fashion. The Judge played by ear, and his music was fluid and beautiful. He'd smile and wink at us while he played, and he'd always call us *"my dear girls"*, and treated us like we were his own children. Shelby told me once that she'd had a dream where Mama admitted to her that the Judge was really her daddy, and told her that she'd be allowed to go and live with the Delacroixs. Shelby wanted to be a Delacroix and I wanted to be a Mitchell, and poor Mama would have been heartbroken had she ever known that. I never knew what Will wanted to be, but it sure wasn't one of us, he left home the first chance he got.

Mama would be thrilled to get a post card from Will, which was good, because it was all she ever got. He never called or visited us since the day he'd left to join the Air Force. When anyone asked about him, Mama would smile sweetly and say, "My Will is off seein' the world, but he'll be back soon enough!" Then she'd show off the picture postcards he'd sent her from places around the globe, talking about the exotic locales as though she'd visited those places herself. Mama clung to the belief that Will would be walking through the door at any given moment, and so she always had his room ready, dusted and polished, with clean linens on his bed. I really think that she believed that Will would be walking through our front door at any moment.

Unfortunately, the next time Will came home was for Mama's funeral, after Rocco Marcucci stabbed her in the heart, which was just moments before I shot him dead with Daddy's police-issue .38.

CHAPTER THREE

Mama had been enamored with Marcucci for a good year and a half, until she realized that she had a 'female problem'. I didn't know it at the time, but found out later through Shelby (who was an expert eavesdropper) that Rocco had given Mama herpes. Mama, being a sweet, naïve, southern belle, had never imagined that she, of all people, would get a venereal disease. She was outraged and horrified, and let Mr. Rocco Marcucci know that his presence was no longer desired anywhere near her vicinity, but nobody told Rocco Marcucci what to do, or what not to do.

Marcucci continued coming over, forcing his way into our house and into Mama's room several times over the next few months. Mama would cry and carry on, and although she'd never admitted it to anyone, we knew he was hurting her. After every one of Marcucci's visits, our fair-skinned mother would be covered in bruises. When we couldn't take it anymore, Shelby and I went to Mama and told her that we knew her secret. She was mortified that anyone would know what a horror her life had become, so she swore us to secrecy. For months we lived with the agony of knowing what was happening to Mama, but were too scared to tell anyone, and also afraid of what would happen to her if we didn't.

Benny would start growling the minute Marcucci's car pulled into our driveway, as a warning that danger was approaching; even the dog had recognized evil when he smelled it. Benny bared his fangs at Marcucci only one time before he mysteriously disappeared while we were at school one day, and we never saw our faithful pet again.

That was the only time that Shelby allowed me to band together with her and her friends, so that we could post notices on every street sign and telephone pole in our town, all while calling Benny's name in vain. Shelby kept reassuring me that we'd find him, that he was probably holed up in someone's garage, or in an abandoned car. Shelby reminded me about the time Daddy was putting an addition on our house, and how Benny had followed us as we rode in Daddy's old truck clear across town to the river, where Daddy illegally dumped his fill dirt. We begged Daddy to please stop, and allow Benny to ride in the truck with us, but Daddy said that he believed that the exercise would do Benny some good. Poor old Benny's paws were bloody by the time we got back home, and I cried while Shelby tended to his wounds, the whole time muttering under her breath about what she'd like to do to that mean, drunken fool. Shelby pointed out that Benny was a tough mutt, and that if he could make it through that, he'd find his way home to us, no matter what. I knew that Shelby was wrong this time; I knew without a doubt that Marcucci had done away with Benny, as I remembered the look in his eyes when Benny had growled at him, it was frightening, a look of pure evil. I think Mama knew it too, although she kept telling us not to worry. She'd said that Benny was the smartest dog in the whole, wide world, and that he'd find his way home to us, but I knew she didn't believe that. I could see the tears shimmering in her eyes as she blinked to keep them from falling. Mama was an actress at heart, but even she wasn't good enough at acting to hide her anguish over the agony she'd brought into our home in the form of an Italian, not-so-gentlemanly, caller.

We stopped inviting friends over, and avoided the neighbors. God forbid someone should wander into the prison our home had become, and find out the truth. By that time Shelby was almost eighteen, and had just graduated from high school. I was fifteen, and had just barely made it out of tenth grade, since turning my attention to the stress of home and forgetting my schoolwork altogether. Shelby was scarce, and I'd spend as much time at Jayne's as Mama would tolerate. I felt guilty about leaving her home alone with that monster, but I just couldn't stay there and listen to the sounds that emanated from her room while he was there. My stomach was constantly in knots, and I was having trouble sleeping. I'd climb out of my bedroom window at night and sit on the garage roof, smoking cigarettes that I didn't inhale just to pass the time.

I was miserable, and Jayne, being my best friend, was always looking for ways to cheer me up. She didn't know the half of what was going on in my life, but she knew that it was bad, and felt that drinking would help to alleviate my pain. Each of us had a reason to drink; I was looking for salvation, and Jayne was looking for the next good time. Jayne and I had always managed to finagle the leftover cocktails that Edith and Charlie would leave around the house, even if it meant chasing vodka with scotch. One time, Jayne managed to borrow two bottles of wine from the cabinet of a musician she'd babysat for. We drank a little each day, managing to make the two bottles last for an entire weekend. The alcohol didn't really alleviate any of my heartache, but at least it made me forget it for just a little while. Sometimes it was only the thought of getting drunk that got me through the day; it was the light at the end of the dark tunnel that my life had become. Jayne's life was roses by comparison, but for some unknown reason, she seemed to need the booze more than I did. Jayne never complained about her life, but seemed bored by it all, and drinking was her diversion.

Shelby and I stayed up late one night thinking up a plan of action, because we knew that Mama wasn't dealing with her situation in a rational manner. We knew that we'd have to go far away, out of the grasp of Marcucci and his band of hoodlums. There was only one person we knew of who would take us all in, no questions asked - our grandfather in Charleston. When we confronted Mama, we told her that we'd have to pack up and leave town in the middle of the night in order to slip away from Marcucci and his goombahs. She flipped out on us.

"Ah refuse to leave mah home and run from this like some kind of criminal! Ah did nothing wrong! Ah will not go back home to Papa Joe like some kind of whipped dog!"

Mama's refusal to go back to Charleston was pure stubborn pride. She told us that her daddy had warned her that Bill Dunne was a drunken Irishman who'd come to no good, and said that if she left Charleston with that no-good Yankee, then she'd better not come back. Being the stubborn, thick-headed girl she was, she refused to ever go home, except to attend her mama's funeral. She told us that she'd survived her drunken Irish husband and now, by God, she was determined that she would survive this no-good, Eye-talian Casanova! Only she didn't.

CHAPTER FOUR

I had dinner at Jayne's after we'd gone to see *Butch Cassidy and the Sundance Kid*. All the way home we pretended to be Butch and Sundance, shooting the bad guys who were hiding around every corner. It was the last time in my young life that I'd ever 'play' anything, but I didn't know that at the time. We laughed and giggled as we reveled in our fantasy, so far removed from the hell that reality had become for me at home.

Edith and Charlie were married now, and were in the process of buying a large home in the upscale town of Smoke Rise, about twenty miles west of Oaklawn. While

I'd been invited to visit any time, I knew this signified the end of whatever happiness I had. Jayne would meet new, rich friends, and have a new, rich-girl life, and I'd be stuck in Nowhereville with my crazy mother and her abusive, gangster boyfriend. Jayne promised that we'd talk every day and that nothing would change, but I knew that everything was changing. My only escape had been hanging out at Jayne's house, going out with Jayne's family, and talking to Jayne, but now there'd be no escape for me. I knew that Jayne meant it when she said I was, and always would be, her best friend, but I also knew that would change when she moved on, went to a new school, and met new friends.

Shelby had informed me the day before that she was moving in with her new boyfriend, Apache Williams, who lived in his parent's garage apartment in Paramus. She'd explained to me that it would be more convenient for her, since she was going to the local community college there, and she didn't own a car. She never mentioned anything about Mama's situation, or Marcucci, or what I would do here alone. I couldn't blame Shelby for taking the first opportunity to escape; after all, there wasn't anything she could do to change the situation, and it wasn't her fault that *I* was trapped like a rat.

When I asked Shelby what she thought I should do, she replied, "It's not my problem anymore, Marra, and I don't want to even think about it!" She was, if nothing else, her mother's daughter.

23

So now I knew that it was my problem, and mine alone. Nobody was going to help me, and nobody was going to rescue Mama from the clutches of the maniac she'd welcomed into our lives. Butch and Sundance weren't going to charge through the front door, guns blazing, and save us from the hell our lives had become. Maybe that's why I enjoyed the movies so much, things always seemed to work out for the best. The good guys always won, and the bad guys were vanquished. My life, however, was *not* a movie and, from my vantage point, there weren't *any* good guys.

Even though Marcucci would hurt Mama in private, publicly, he'd hold her hand, smile sweetly, and wine and dine her. Worst of all, she'd act as though she adored him! Mama made me vow not to tell anyone the truth: "Nevah, evah, divulge the ugliness of what mah life has become, Marra darlin', cause Ah jus could not live with that!" As it turned out, she really didn't have to worry about that much longer.

Jayne saw the tears in my eyes when I said goodbye to her that night, and grabbed me in a bear-hug.

"You'll always be my very best friend, Marra! We'll always stay in touch, silly girl! Please don't cry!"

I hugged her back tightly, and professed to believe everything she'd said, but I knew it wasn't true. If only we were older, if only we were graduating, and going off to college together, none of it would matter. But two years is an eternity when you're fifteen – it feels like forever.

I walked home in the dreary drizzle, alone and lonely. From Jayne's apartment on Donor Avenue to my house on Greenway Terrace, I looked down at the dirty sidewalks and thought about how much my life sucked, and how there were no prospects of it getting better any time soon. Maybe, I thought, I should run away by myself, head south to Papa Joe; I knew he'd take me in. It had been years since we'd visited Charleston, and I'd loved the town and the people. It was interesting that my mother's accent annoyed the crap out of me in New Jersey, but in South Carolina it seemed just fine.

I wondered why Mama hadn't taken us girls and gone back to her daddy when we'd asked - no, begged her. I wondered why she couldn't have put our best interest ahead of her own stupid pride. Shelby was gone now, and Mama didn't have a job, or anything else to tie her down here. I knew that I'd have to give her an ultimatum when I got home. I'd tell her that if she wouldn't leave with me, I would go alone. I made the decision on my way home from Jayne's that come hell or high water, I'd find a way to get to Charleston, with or without Mama. With Shelby gone and me going, she'd have no choice, she'd have to leave town and that beast she'd gotten tangled up with. By the time I got to my street, I'd made up my mind. I had a firm goal now, and the future was beginning to look a little brighter. I could feel my mood lifting.

25

When I turned the corner onto Greenway, I saw the big, gold Cadillac parked in our driveway, and I cringed. My stomach started to churn, and I fought the urge to turn around and go back to Jayne's, or just keep walking somewhere, anywhere, until the creep's car was gone. I contemplated my options as I slowly approached the house, but then I heard Mama's scream, and I bolted to the front door.

In my state of panic it took me a few seconds to realize that I was trying to open a locked door, the handle unyielding in my hand. When it sunk in that the door was locked, I ran around to the back door, which stood open, with shards of glass all around it on the ground. My first thought was that someone had broken in, but Marcucci's car was here. Had *he* been the one to break the glass door? I stepped over the glass and entered the house, tiptoeing through the family room, kitchen and hallway, quietly approaching Mama's room. I heard her talking softly, her voice pleading.

"Please don't, Rocco, please, Ah beg you! Ah have mah babies who need me! Please don't!" And then she screamed, "No!"

I sprinted to the hall closet and scaled my way up the shelves to the top. My hand was searching blindly beneath the old sheets and pillowcases until I felt the cold metal of Daddy's gun, nestled there beneath the pile of linens, right where he'd always kept it.

Years before, Daddy had made a big deal out of showing us the gun, and where it was hidden. He'd taught us all to shoot, and said that it was only for a dire emergency – if he ever caught any of us playing with it, we'd be sorry. Daddy was a mean drunk who'd whip your hide for looking at him the wrong way, so none of us ever considered messing with that gun. It had been years since I'd even thought about that gun, but instinctively, in my fear and panic, I'd headed right for it, and there it was!

I grabbed the heavy gun, and with my finger on the trigger, I bolted down the hallway toward Mama's room. I didn't know if the gun was loaded, or what I intended to do with it, but that didn't stop my progress. It was as though my brain had shut down, and my body was on auto-pilot. Through the crack in the open door I saw Marcucci with his back to me. He was standing over Mama's bloody body, and a large kitchen knife protruded out of her chest, while her wide-open eyes stared blindly at the ceiling.

I pushed the door open and Marcucci spun around, saying, "She asked for it! I told her if she ever locked me out again . . . "

BANG. The sound was louder than I'd anticipated, much louder than the guns that Butch and Sundance had fired in the movie. The discharge jolted my shoulder, and I let the gun drop onto the faux Persian carpet that Mama had covered her wooden floor with. One shot, but it had been a good one - right between the eyes. Daddy had always said that if you're going to shoot, you shoot to kill - don't mess around. I remembered him saying, "Always go for the head shot, Marra. You don't want to wound him; he'll only kill you if you do that!" I was only seven at the time, and Daddy's statement had made an indelible impact. My very first thought after pulling the trigger was that I should have done this yesterday, while Mama was still alive.

I stepped over Marcucci, and knelt down next to my mother's lifeless body. I skimmed Mama's cheek with my fingertips, as her eyes stared blindly toward the heavens. Her face was warm, and her lilac scent filled the room. A single tear ran from her right, gold-flecked, green eye, into her wavy, chestnut-colored hairline. I thought that perhaps she'd survive this, and that maybe this time tomorrow we'd be headed for Charleston, just the two of us. Mama's *Sugar-Coral* lipstick was applied perfectly, as usual, and her long, curly lashes gleamed from the light shining down from the ceiling fixture. I could see the faint dusting of powdered makeup over her tiny, turned-up nose. The rosy blush she'd applied to her high cheek bones like a professional artist stood out in contrast to her pale skin. In that moment, I thought that she was the most beautiful woman I'd ever seen.

Although I knew in my heart she was already dead, I said, "Mama?" just in case I was wrong. I leaned over her and hugged her one last time, covering myself in her warm blood. I waited a few seconds, and then looked into her green eyes and said, "I'm going to go and call the police now, Mama. It'll be okay, you just stay right here, and I'll take care of everything, I promise."

I stepped over Marcucci's corpse without so much as a glance and walked into the kitchen, picked up the wall phone, and dialed the police phone number that was etched in my memory from years of calling Daddy at work.

"This is Marra Dunne on Greenway Terrace, and I have two dead people here in my house. Could you please send someone over, sir?"

I hung up the phone, went out the front door, and sat down on the steps, and I waited for them to come and take me away.

CHAPTER FIVE

As I heard the sirens approaching, I saw the neighbors begin popping their heads out of doors to see what the commotion was. The closer the sirens came, the more neighbors came out. By the time the black and white pulled up in front of my house, it seemed like the entire neighborhood was out in full force. It was like a block party without any real party. The neighbors were talking to one another, and possibly talking to me, too, but I couldn't decipher their words. Mouths moved and fingers pointed, but I didn't know what they were saying. It was as though I was in another dimension from the rest of them.

The first two cops to arrive on the scene were young, and I was as unfamiliar to them as they were to me. I'm sure they knew that this was Bill Dunne's house, or at least that it used to be. Small town cops all know each other, even the ones who retired before they came onto the force, at least by reputation. They came over to me casually, as if it were a routine call. Seeing them approach brought my world back into focus.

"Miss?" asked one of the officers, "Did you call in to the station? Is there a problem?"

"Not anymore," I said softly, not bothering to look up at them.

"Why did you call the police? What did you tell the dispatcher? Did you tell him there were bodies in your house?" he persisted.

It was then I looked up into his clear, blue eyes, and stated plainly, "Yes. My mother's boyfriend stabbed her to death, and I shot him. But I was too late to save her; it's too late for her."

My head dropped back down slowly and I stared at the ground, which seemed to be spinning wildly. I wasn't dizzy, or ill, in fact, I felt nothing at all, but the ground seemed to be spinning out of control. I'm not sure what happened next. I think they left me there on the steps alone and went around me, through the front door, and into the house. Eventually, they came back out, and one of them sat next to me, while the other one headed back to the patrol car, talking into the radio to some unknown entity. I'm not sure how long I sat there with that young policeman at my side, and though I couldn't really see him, I could feel his leg pressed against mine, and his arm around my back and my shoulders. He was speaking, but I didn't know if it was directed at me or someone else. His voice was calm, serene, and soothing, like a melody. I imagined he was singing me a lullaby, like I was a baby, and he was my daddy. The sirens broke my reverie, as more police cars and more people arrived at the scene. Finally, the young cop who'd been sitting next to me rose and said, "C'mon, honey, let's get you into the car."

I got up and leaned into him, as he slowly led me to the car, where he opened the back door, and gently helped me in. Neighbors were craning their necks, trying to see me better in my blood-spattered outfit, but they'd been warned to stay back, away from the police car. The young policeman stood next to the open door for a while, every so often peeking into the back seat to check on me. Finally he asked, "Sweetheart, is there anyone I can call for you? Grandparents? Relatives?"

"No," I said, believing that I was alone in the world. I was thinking that nobody cared about me anymore, and even if anyone did, they couldn't help me now, anyway. Eventually, he closed the door and walked away. There I sat, alone, in the dark, not thinking, not feeling, and seeing nothing - except for the flashing red strobe of the bubble gum machine that sat atop the black and white. That's what we called it when we were little and Daddy used to bring his patrol car home, the bubble gum machine. And there I sat, until Marcucci's brother came, threatening to kill me.

PART II

1975, Age 21

Getting Away With Murder

I awake in a hospital bed. The lights are low, and my head is spinning. The antiseptic smell is stinging my nose, and my arm is aching where the IV needle is inserted. I seem to be alone with only grief for company, and I can't immediately call to mind the details that brought me here. I know it must stem from the consequences of my own actions, because I have killed again. The main difference is that this time it was premeditated, but there were no legal repercussions. I was simply allowed to walk away, free as a bird, carrying only the unimaginable guilt, grief, and pain that have haunted me since that fateful day.

So much has happened since I've been back on the outside . . .

CHAPTER SIX

Three years before . . .

The day I turned eighteen, I was released from the Maria Benoit Juvenile Detention Center for Girls. It had been my home for two and a half years, and while it was no picnic, it wasn't all bad either. I'd finished my high school equivalency there, and I was half-way through an associate's degree by the time I was released. I'd made a few friends, and learned some valuable lessons about the nature of human beings.

Although the Marcucci family had petitioned to have me tried as an adult and locked up for life (or released into the wild as prey for their hunting pleasure), Judge Delacroix actually carried more weight with the prosecutor's office than did the slimy, junior Mafiosi Marcuccis of Bergen County.

The Judge had been my very first visitor in lockup the night that Mama was murdered and I'd put an end to Marcucci's miserable existence. The Judge's first words to me were, "Oh, my poor, dear girl, I am so sorry for what has happened to you!"

It surprised me to realize that there was someone who believed in me, and would actually help me in my hour of need. Before the Judge had arrived at the Oaklawn Police Station, where I was being held pending instruction from the County Prosecutor's office, I'd assumed that I was going to jail for life. After all, I'd admitted to killing a sub-human, so prison would be my fate, and I'd have to accept it. Then the Judge arrived, so full of kindness and compassion, telling me that he understood what had happened *to* me. He'd told me that he wished that I had come to him for help a long time ago. Judge Delacroix seemed to know a lot about what had been going on, and I found out later that he'd spoken with Shelby about our family saga before coming to see me. The Judge vowed to help me, and to try to keep me out of prison, and for that I was grateful. But I was even more grateful for his understanding. It had been a very long time since anyone had made me feel protected.

During the two and a half years I had been incarcerated a lot had happened 'on the outside', as inmates say. Shelby had married Apache, who was now using his Christian name, Albert, and she'd given birth to a baby girl named Darcy Charlotte Williams. They lived with Albert's parents while he attended classes at Paterson State College, and worked part-time with his father, who owned the Firestone Tire Center on Route 4. Shelby's mother-in-law was a doting grandmother, and was like a mother to Shelby. I was happy for Shelby, she'd finally found her perfect family, and they had the money and status befitting her beauty and talent. Although her visits to me had been sporadic at best, I understood that she had responsibilities in her life now, and that she was trying to 'get over' all that had happened.

"After all, Marra," she'd said, "I didn't kill anybody, so why should I have to suffer for it?"

"You're right," I said, "I put myself here, so you don't have to worry about visiting me – I don't really have much time for visitors anyway."

Shelby seemed relieved to hear that, and only came to see me once more, on my seventeenth birthday.

Jayne, on the other hand, visited once a month like clockwork, even though she had to travel from Smoke

Rise, and then, after she'd started college, from Boston. She'd always apologize for not coming more often, and I'd always tell her that I was grateful that she hadn't forgotten me, and that she showed up at all. Edith and Charlie came regularly as well, bringing me gifts of food, clothing, and books. They, too, apologized for not realizing what a desperate situation I'd been in. They said that they would have done something to help, if only they'd known, but I don't think that anyone could have changed the course of events. God knows, I'd been over it in my mind a thousand times. Mama was who she was, and she wasn't going to listen to anyone about anything, even if it meant the death of her.

Judge Delacroix came to visit me twice a week, on Wednesdays and Sundays. We'd play card games on Wednesdays with two of the other inmates. They were nice girls who had found themselves in unfortunate circumstances, and who were now paying for their poor choices. On Sundays, the Judge and I played chess; he'd taught me to play, and after about six months I started to best him. The first time I was able to utter the word "checkmate" was quite exhilarating, and a real sense of accomplishment. I believe that the Judge was just as pleased as I was at my success.

A few of the inmates asked why my judge was spending so much time with me. I'd explained that he hadn't been my juvenile court judge, that his name was Judge – which of course wasn't true, but on the inside you never reveal too much of yourself, it's not healthy. I had seen girls beaten up because they wouldn't share their cigarettes or candy. They were the girls who would flaunt what they had like they used to on the outside, thinking that the same rules applied in here – that if you had more than the next guy, you were somehow better than them. Wrong move behind the iron curtain! You show off in a place like that and you're going to get taken down a notch or two real quickly; Shelby wouldn't have lasted a day. Those of us who were incarcerated for murder were afforded status, and therefore left alone. It was like opposite world, the worse they deemed you to be, the higher up the totem pole you were placed.

The Judge promised that I could come and live with him when I was released, and said that he'd send me to college and help me *'move past this tragedy'*. He painted a picture of a rosy future, and I found myself looking forward to beginning my life anew, with a real, caring father, who was looking out for me.

The Judge was a tall man, six feet, four inches, and had the kindest blue eyes I'd ever seen. He moved and spoke slowly, and with purpose. His demeanor immediately put you at ease, and you'd feel a sense of peace around him. I would imagine how different my life would have been had I been born a Delacroix rather than a Dunne, and knew that I never would have ended up where I was. In some of my daydreams Shelby was my Delacroix sister, but in most, I was an only child. Try as I might, I just couldn't imagine a scenario where my sister Shelby was kind to me, so since they were my daydreams I chose to leave her out of them.

Daddy had shown up right after the incident and professed his sobriety. He said that he was now and forever back in our lives, and promised to stand by me throughout my ordeal, but two days later he totaled his car on Route 46 while intoxicated. After his release from Hackensack Medical Center he went to live with his brother in Michigan, and I never heard from him again.

My brother Will came back for Mama's funeral, a tall, thin soldier in uniform. He sat off to the side, like a stranger who'd mistakenly wandered in off the street. You couldn't see his face as he sat slumped over, head in hands, sandy hair covering his blue, watering eyes. He hugged both Shelby and me before he left the service, but said very little, except that he was sorry. I wasn't sure what he was sorry about, and I didn't ask him. He never came to visit me inside the JDC, but sent picture postcards from exotic locales. The same thing was written on every one, *Dear Marra, Hope you're doing okay. Wish you were here. Love, Will* - the very same thing he'd written on each of Mama's postcards, except of course, they began *Dear Mama.* The double r's in Marra looked almost identical to the second m in Mama, so Will's life hadn't really changed that much. I couldn't blame him for wanting to escape the insanity, but I'd secretly wished that he'd stayed close by and had been around to visit me once in a while.

CHAPTER SEVEN

I'd made friends with a few girls while I was incarcerated, and one in particular, Cynthia Brady (although she insisted we just call her Brady), became a close friend. She had also killed her mother's boyfriend, she'd told me with tears flowing from her big, dark, doe-eyes, but her mother was still living. After two years of being raped by him on her mother's Bingo nights, Brady had killed him with a steak knife to the gut. That particular scumbag's name was George Carbello, who was, interestingly enough, related to the Marcucci family by marriage. I'm sure that the Marcuccis would have loved to get their hands on Brady and me upon our release.

The saddest thing for Brady was that her mother had turned against her, and had accused Brady of ruining *her* life. Her mother wasn't at all concerned that Brady had been raped repeatedly by this scumbag from the day she turned thirteen, her only concern was that she no longer had a meal ticket.

When I'd hear stories like Brady's from the girls inside I'd feel better about my own life, lame as it was. Brady's greatest loss was the same as mine - her mother. Only I think it was worse for her, because at least I could console myself with the fact that although my mother was dead, she had loved me, Brady couldn't. I'd like to believe that had I been in the situation Brady was in, Miss Charlotte would have been the one to plunge the knife into the bastard who had raped her daughter.

Many of the girls who were incarcerated with me had been molested by someone in, or close to, their own families. Most of them believed that their mothers knew what was happening to them all along, and did nothing to prevent it. This was real life, not an afternoon TV movie special where some hero flies in and saves the damsel in distress. No Butch and Sundance to save us - we were all just children left to our own devices to combat the evil we'd faced.

All of us had been damaged in some way by the people who were supposed to love and protect us from monsters, monsters that they'd brought into our lives.

Some of the girls became as mean as their abusers and took their aggression out on others, but most of us retreated into a protective shell and kept our own secrets from the world.

Six weeks before my eighteenth birthday, and my release, my social worker, Mrs. Gray, escorted me into her office and asked me to sit down. I had a bad feeling, like maybe she was going to tell me that they'd changed their minds and decided to send me to adult prison for the rest of my life. I could see in her face that something bad was about to happen, and tried to brace myself.

"Marra, I'm so very sorry to have to give you this awful news. I know how close you were with Judge Delacroix, and I'm so sorry to inform you that the Judge passed away this morning from a heart attack . . . his housekeeper found him. Marra . . . did you hear me? Marra, the Judge is dead."

The Judge is dead, the Judge is dead, the Judge is dead - all the way back to my room it was repeating in my head. Following me to my door, Mrs. Gray kept asking if I was okay, if I needed anything, or if I wanted to talk. Yeah, Mrs. Gray, I want to talk to the Judge.

I sat on my bed alone for what seemed like an eternity, until Brady came in looking for me.

"Hey, Marra, what's up? What's wrong? Why are you crying?"

I hadn't realized that I'd been crying until I heard Brady's question, and it caused me to remember the testimony of the young cop at my hearing, the one who had sat next to me on my front steps and then escorted me into the back seat of the police car.

"She was visibly upset, shaking and crying the entire time," he'd said.

I hadn't know that a person could be shaking and crying and be unaware of it. I thought perhaps I should ask Mrs. Gray about that, because she seemed to care about me, but maybe that was an act that social workers learn in social worker school. The only thing of value I'd learned from her was the Serenity Prayer; we had to recite it at the beginning of each group meeting with her.

'God grant me the serenity to accept the things I cannot change; courage to change the things I can; and wisdom to know the difference.

Living one day at a time; Enjoying one moment at a time; Accepting hardships as the pathway to peace; Taking, as He did, this sinful world as it is, not as I would have it; Trusting that He will make all things right if I surrender to His Will; That I may be reasonably happy in this life, and supremely happy with Him Forever in the next. Amen.'

It was basically a load of crap, but like any other mantra that is repeated enough, after a while you zone out and forget why you're depressed. I eventually found a short cut for it in my own mind, *'Let it be'*, and then would just call to mind the Beatle's song, and hear it playing in my head.

"The Judge is dead," I told Brady, as I looked up into her big, dark eyes.

Within the hour the news had spread, and my room was filled with the girls I'd gotten to know pretty well since I'd been inside. Most of them were telling me how sorry they were to hear that my dad had died, and to me, it was worse than if it *had* been my dad. The Judge had been the father to me that my own father had never been. Life sucks, and then you die. Not quite eighteen yet, and that was my life's motto.

I was allowed to attend the Judge's funeral, but only with Mrs. Gray along as my chaperone. She seemed to constantly be holding on to me, either my shoulder, my arm, or my hand. I wasn't sure if she was trying to be consoling, or if she was just trying to prevent me from flying the coop.

CHAPTER EIGHT

My 'Custodial Advocate', Mr. Palmer, went over all of the paperwork I had to sign upon my release. A lot of girls had to be on probation after they were released, but the Judge had seen to it that when I was released my juvenile record would be expunged, as if nothing had ever happened. Yeah, tell that to my memory!

Mr. Palmer told me that the Judge had named me as a beneficiary of his estate, but that it was still in probate and being contested by a nephew from Pennsylvania. There was also an irrevocable trust the Judge had set up for me that was 'outside of the purview' of the estate, whatever that meant. Mr. Palmer explained that there were funds available for my living expenses and education that could be obtained though the Judge's attorney, Mr. Thomas Davis of Dewey, Davis and Pope. He gave me Mr. Davis's business card, and told me to set up a meeting with him at my earliest convenience.

I walked out of the front gate of the Maria Benoit Juvenile Detention Center with one small suitcase and thought, '*Free at last, free at last, good God Almighty, I'm free at last!*' I scanned the street looking for Jayne's '73 candy-apple red Mustang convertible. I spotted her parked at the corner, waving to me with both hands.

"Over here! C'mon, Marra – hurry up, we've got places to go and people to meet!"

Jayne looked wonderful, dressed in jeans and a tight blue sweater. Her hair was full of blonde highlights, and her makeup looked like it had been applied by a professional. Jayne had always been rather plain looking and I'd always felt kind of sorry for her, having such a glamorous mother to compare herself to, but now she looked more like Edith than ever. She had Edith's blue eyes and straight Patrician nose, but not her full lips; Jayne's mouth was a straight slash of thin lips, but when she smiled, her face lit up like Christmas, and her eyes had that kindness that turned the ice-blue warm. She was more like a sister to me than my own sister was, and I felt lucky to have her and her family in my life.

I spent most of the first four months of my freedom with Edith and Charlie after Jayne had returned to Boston College for classes. Their house was a fabulous six bedroom, four bath, with a fireplace, pool and spa, nestled in the side of a mountain. From the upstairs balcony it felt like a tree-house, a fortress among the towering oaks, elms, and silver birch trees. There was a stream coursing through the woods outside that ran down into a brook in the valley below. When it was quiet at night, you could hear the water babbling as it navigated its way through the rocks and stones. It was peaceful there during the week, in stark contrast to most weekends.

When Jayne was home she'd drag me to bars and clubs to listen to live music, dance, and drink. She did most of the dancing and drinking while I sat at the table, in awe of the activity around me. Jayne seemed oblivious to the guys watching us when she'd drag me onto the dance floor, shimmying around me, saying, *"Come on, Marra, loosen up!"* I was self-conscious and awkward around people, especially guys, but Jayne, on the other hand, seemed to relish being the center of attention. What an odd couple we were.

I would try to sober Jayne up before we'd leave because I couldn't drive, having missed that rite of passage while I'd been locked away. Many times I'd be chanting that Serenity Prayer in my head as we swerved along the mountain roads at high speeds, narrowly missing trees and boulders, not to mention the occasional deer. It was a beautiful, quiet area, and when Jayne was away at school, I didn't have to do anything, but, as Edith would say, 'rest, and compose myself'. That meant sitting out on the deck hammock with a good book. Edith took me to Short Hills Mall and insisted on buying me a complete wardrobe and a makeover at a posh salon. I argued that there was no point in purchasing all of the products that the stylist had applied to my face and hair because I didn't have the first clue how to apply it all, but Edith maintained that these were essentials and that she'd teach me how to use them. I'd gone into the mall looking like a child and came out looking like a younger, hipper version of my mother, whom Edith had always compared to actress Lesley Ann Warren. It was the first time I'd ever heard a wolf whistle that was directed at me.

My dull, lifeless curls were shining, and my thick eyebrows had been plucked into stylish curves over green eyes that now looked twice the size, with the help of shadow, liner, and mascara. Beige linen pants that I'd thought were far too long for me were just the perfect length, now that I teetered on four-inch heels. The neckline of the peasant-style silk chemise revealed more cleavage than I liked, but Edith insisted that it was totally appropriate for a young lady my age. Edith and Charlie cooed over me that night as we dined at Piccolos, their favorite local Italian eatery. I had to admit that I did look fantastic, but I didn't feel like myself – I felt like a child playing dress-up.

The next day Edith took me to meet with the lawyer, Tom Davis, where she did all the talking, questioning him as though she were my legal counsel. She ordered him to send me a checkbook so that I could have assets available should I need anything, although up to that point she hadn't let me spend a penny. Mr. Davis explained that any education costs would be paid for directly by him to my school of choice, and that I'd have access to a monthly stipend for my living expenses. Edith expressed outrage over this, but I thought it was more than generous, and I was thrilled to have been given anything at all.

At Edith's insistence I called Shelby and arranged to meet her and my baby niece at a restaurant on Route 4, near her home. Shelby reluctantly agreed, saying she didn't want any trouble. Trouble? What did she think I was going to do, shoot her? I just wanted to see her, and even more so, meet the baby. I'd been hoping that things would be different between us. Now that we were older, and Shelby was a mom, I thought that our relationship would be better. I hoped that Shelby and I would become close, and maybe be able to be friends, as well as sisters.

When we got to the restaurant, Shelby was already seated, and seemed uncomfortable and antsy. She looked the same, pretty as ever, and she'd even complimented me on how I looked, saying, "Marra, if I didn't know it was you, I wouldn't have believed it!"

I assumed it to be a compliment judging by the expression on her face, though she didn't actually say I looked nice. She didn't get up to greet us, but remained seated and continued flipping through her menu, as if we met weekly, and this was no big deal. Edith looked at me with raised eyebrows and a tight smile, obviously unhappy with Shelby's unfriendly demeanor.

The baby was adorable, and insisted on sitting on my lap most of the time, which delighted me and mortified Shelby. Darcy's chubby little fingers kept grabbing at the gold hoops dangling from my earlobes, finally popping one out, causing her to shriek with laughter. I took the other one out as well and let her play with them, being careful that she didn't eat them. Shelby kept apologizing for Darcy bothering me, even though I'd insisted that I loved every minute of it. Although baby Darcy and I had never met, we bonded instantly. It could have been because we were each experiencing life outside for the first time; for her outside the womb, and for me outside of a prison. I felt like I could have held her forever and been happy doing nothing else.

"I don't understand it, Marra, she never takes to strangers!" Shelby stated.

"But my dear," Edith informed her coolly, "Marra is *not* a stranger, she's Darcy's auntie!"

I'm sure it wasn't lost on Shelby that the baby looked more like me than she did her. Darcy had the same round, green eyes, small nose, and little cleft in her chin that I had. Her hair was dark and curly, like mine, whereas Shelby's was blonde and poker-straight. Darcy was quick to smile, and seemed to delight in holding my face in her hands. I felt my heart fill up with love for this little girl, and wished that I could scoop her up and run away. Although Darcy was delighted, her mother seemed disinterested, and even distracted. Shelby didn't have much to say, and if it hadn't been for Edith, who carried the conversation, it would have been a quiet luncheon.

When we left, Shelby was standing miserably in the parking lot holding a wailing baby, who held her chubby arms out to me as if pleading for me to take her along. It broke my heart to leave that baby, and I said a silent prayer that Shelby would warm towards me so that I could have a relationship with them both.

Edith could read the sadness on my face, and put her hand on my leg to comfort me, and then suggested that we visit George Washington Memorial Park, where my mother's body had been interred. She stopped at a florist shop and bought a beautiful bouquet for me to leave at Mama's gravesite.

I was surprised to see a granite marker in the ground with Mama's name, dates of birth and death, and the words 'Loving Mother' inscribed on it. In all this time it had never occurred to me that Mama had a grave somewhere, a place where I could go and visit her, even though I'd been there when they'd lowered her casket into the ground. I'd had dreams about her, dreams where she would talk to me, and tell me how sorry she was for everything that had happened, but I hadn't been able to talk to her. Maybe I could do that here.

Edith went back to her car and left me alone there for a while to visit. I sat on the ground next to the marker, rubbing bits of dirt and grass off of it, and circling the letters of her name with my fingers.

"Mama, I'm glad I killed him. I'm sorry that you had to die just for being dumb, but I'm glad I killed him for you. I don't know why you stayed with him; I don't know why you wouldn't run away with us. There are so many things I don't know, Mama, but I aim to find out."

I sat there for a while, looking around at the park-like setting, thinking about how pretty and peaceful this place was, and knowing that I'd never come back here again. There wasn't anything else to say.

CHAPTER NINE

At the end of the summer, when Jayne was getting ready to return to Boston for the start of a new semester, I made a decision about what to do next. Edith wanted me to stay with her and Charlie and take classes locally. She thought I needed to be nurtured a bit longer before going out into the cold, cruel world, but I knew it was time for me to take the next step. Brady was about to be sprung from the JDC, and she and I had made plans to live together for a while until we figured out what to do with the rest of our lives.

Once Edith realized that she couldn't convince me to stay, she helped me pack my things, and fussed over me, and talked about having some kind of going away party. I really didn't want a bunch of strangers that I didn't know, acting like it was a big deal for me to be leaving a place that I didn't belong in anyway, so I resisted. Edith finally gave up, and she and Charlie settled for taking me out for one last dinner together. I sat through two hours of advice on what to do if . . .

I thanked them both profusely for all of their kindness, and left the next day with mixed emotions. On one hand, I felt a sense of freedom and adventure, and on the other, a sense of fear of the vast unknown that lay ahead of me now.

I met Brady at the bus stop on Route 4 in Elmwood Park, where Edith had dropped me. Brady 'oohed' and 'aahed' over how fantastic I looked, and then said that she wanted to stop and see her mother one last time before we headed south. When I'd asked her why she wanted to go and see the woman who had never once visited her the entire time she'd been incarcerated, she said she needed some kind of closure.

From the bus stop, we walked down the Boulevard to Mrs. Brady's apartment, an end unit in a complex of hundreds of brick buildings where children played in courtyards and dogs barked through open windows. The woman took her sweet time answering the door, and then feigned surprise to see Brady standing there.

"Cynthia! What in the world are you doing here? I thought you were in prison!" the bleached-blonde bimbo exclaimed.

"No, Mom, it wasn't prison, it was Juvenile Detention, and I'm out. I'm eighteen, in case you've forgotten, and I'm free now," Brady told her in a deadpan voice.

No hug, no kiss, just, "Well, what do you want from me? You can't stay here, and certainly not with a friend!" Brady's mother said, eyeing me with distain while she popped her gum, and blew a cloud of cigarette smoke in my face.

Brady and I turned to look at one another and started giggling, which turned to laughter, and then, on her part, to tears.

"Well, thanks for nothing, and fuck you, Mom!" Brady said, and then turned, and hopped down the two-step stoop.

The woman leered at me viciously, pursing her red-stained lips, waiting to see what I'd have to say.

"Yeah," I said, "Fuck you, Mrs. Brady!" I heard the door slam after I'd turned away, and I fought the urge to go back and kick it for good measure. I wasn't mad at her for myself, but for Brady. How hurtful, to have your own mother treat you like a piece of dirt!

I had my arm around Brady for the next few blocks as we headed toward Route 46, and the bus that was heading south toward Asbury Park, and the cheapest rent on the Jersey shore. Brady had been crying at first, but then suddenly, started laughing.

"What the hell are you laughing about, Brady?"

"Fuck you, Mrs. Brady! That was great, Marra! I didn't know you had it in you!" she said, and we went on laughing and giggling for the rest of walk.

We ate at Pizza Town USA, and then boarded the bus, stuffed to the gills and armed with a bag of zeppoles for the hour ride south. It was scary not knowing where we were going to end up, but it was also exciting to have the freedom to be traveling into that unknown.

"You know what we need, Marra?" Brady asked, as she stuffed a zeppole into her mouth, covering her face with powdered sugar in the process.

"What's that, Brady?" I asked, chuckling at the sight of her powdered face.

"We need new names, new last names. We're starting over, going where nobody knows us, and we need to reinvent ourselves. We could use the same last name, and tell people that we're sisters."

"We're not going that far, Brady."

We would have, and while I could have, Brady could not legally leave the state of New Jersey because she was on probation until she turned twenty-one. I'd promised Brady that I wouldn't abandon her, and I was all she had in this world, she needed me.

"Okay, then," I agreed, "Let's think of a new last name."

We came up with names like Morrison, for Jim, and Hendrix, for Jimi, even Joplin, for Janis, but none of them sounded just right. Then we started with places, like Boston, Denver, and Detroit, when the guy in the seat behind us said, *"Dallas."*

We simultaneously turned to face him, a ruddy-faced, old guy, with wire-rimmed glasses and a shock of white hair. He looked like Santa without the beard.

"Dallas!" he smiled, through huge, gapped, white teeth.

"That's where I'm from originally, beautiful country, just beautiful, like you girls! I think you should call yourselves the Dallas Sisters!" he exclaimed, grinning from ear to ear.

He must have thought we were singers trying to come up with a stage name, not ex-cons trying to begin a new life. He was so convincing that we had to agree. Brady Dallas and Marra Dallas sounded like good, real names. So Dallas it was, and as soon as we had enough money we went to court and had our names changed legally. I only had to change my last name, but Brady had to change both, dropping the 'Cynthia' in favor of her current last name as her new first name. It seemed to fit her, and she beamed with pride as she read the legal decree.

CHAPTER TEN

Our apartment was on the corner of Sunset and Grand in beautiful, dilapidated Asbury Park. Ours was one of two apartments on the first floor of what was once an old estate home, just a few blocks from the ocean and Convention Hall. There was a basement apartment that housed the owner's demented mother-in-law, a little, old Italian lady who was always dressed in black. Bruce Springsteen's cousin lived in the apartment across the hall from us, but we didn't know who Bruce was then, so we were unimpressed by his cousin. There were two apartments on the second floor, one occupied by an older woman who seldom spoke to anyone, and the other occupied by a pretty young woman in her twenties who was a legal secretary. The entire third floor had been made into a lovely apartment to house the owner's son and his new bride, they were a handsome young couple. Dino looked like a linebacker for the Jets, and Donna was a petite, cool blonde with a turned-up nose.

Brady and I immediately scored jobs in the restaurant downtown that was owned by our landlady. Brady was hired as a server and I was hired as a cook, having gained culinary experience 'inside'. I made up a clever name of a restaurant on my job application, and fortunately, nobody bothered to ask any questions. It turned out to be a good thing for us; the landlady gave us a discount on our rent, and Dino drove us to work every day, since he was going there anyway. I'm not sure that his wife was thrilled about the arrangement, but she had no room to talk. More than once I'd seen Donna bringing male company up the massive staircase to their apartment, holding hands, and giggling all the way. It made me uncomfortable to have this information, but it wasn't any of my business. Besides, Dino did an extraordinary amount of flirting with every female who came within spitting distance.

Brady started dating Freddie, the scraggly kid who worked as a short-order cook by day, and played in a band at night. He was nice enough, and really cute, but kind of scrawny and greasy, like he couldn't wash the French fry oil out of his hair. He'd hit on me a few times in the kitchen, but I let him know I wasn't interested. I guess he figured if he couldn't have me, one sister was as good as the other. I never did tell Brady that he'd chosen me first, it would have hurt her feelings, and she was insecure enough as it was.

I had become enamored with reading while I was incarcerated; it helped pass the time, and took me away to another place and time, where I didn't have to deal with my own reality. The massive mahogany staircase in our building was set in the center hall, where bookshelves lined every surrounding wall of the cavernous entryway. There must have been a library in the original layout of the old house that had been cleared out to make one of the apartment units, and the bookshelves had been relocated. The assortment of reading material was eclectic, but I wasn't choosy; I read Erle Stanley Gardner, Kurt Vonnegut, Silvia Plath, Ken Kesey, J.D. Salinger, C.S. Lewis, John Updike, Ernest Hemingway, Taylor Caldwell, Irwin Shaw, and every other book on those bookshelves. When I'd exhausted the supply, I acquainted myself with the Asbury Park Library.

I'd noticed the very tall, dark librarian with the pony tail observing me on several occasions. He looked like Frank Zappa, and his huge, heavily-lidded eyes followed my every move, though he never said a word. After three months of him visually stalking me, I decided to take the bull by the horns, and went over to ask him a question. I could see that he was unnerved by my approach by the way his big, dark eyes shifted toward and away from me. I was glad, because that gave me the upper hand with him, he seemed more shy and uncertain than I was. I felt bold and adventurous as I was about to step into what was new, and unchartered territory for me, flirtation. I'd witnessed Jayne do it often enough, so I decided to mimic her act. It wasn't me, but truthfully, I had no idea what *was* me.

"Excuse me," I whispered, "Can you tell me if you have the book *Everything You've Ever Wanted to Know About Sex, but Were Afraid to Ask?*" It was a pretty bold maneuver for a nineteen-year-old, ex-con virgin.

His eyes widened, and then his mouth relaxed into a smile. He was really quite handsome, although a tad on the skinny side.

"Sure," he replied, "follow me."

"Are you going to show me to the book, or are you going to show me something else?" I asked, with as much sincerity as I could muster.

With a huge grin, he turned to me and said, "Which would you prefer, miss?"

We started dating not long after that first encounter, and he was my entry into womanhood, and a very fine one indeed. His name was James Logan, a 29-year-old, divorced father of two, Vietnam veteran, with a Master's degree in Library Sciences. He was eerily quiet, and looked like a character who might live in a haunted house, complete with cobwebs and dark tunnels. Brady said he looked emaciated, like someone who had spent time in a concentration camp.

"Why don't you fatten him up?" she'd asked, "You're a great cook, and he looks like he'd be quite handsome with an additional forty pounds!"

She wanted me to invite him over, but I never did. Our relationship was compartmentalized - I never shared my personal story with him, and he never shared his with me. All I knew about him was that he'd been stationed in England, where he'd married his pregnant girlfriend. Not long after the baby was born, James had been sent to Vietnam, where he found out by mail that his wife was pregnant again, and filing for divorce. She still lived there with his two children and her new husband. When his tour of duty ended, James returned home to his parents in New Jersey, accepting defeat, and letting her go without a fight - which seemed to jibe with his basic personality - the path of least resistance.

James moved to Asbury Park after getting the job as head librarian. He lived in a small apartment in a house not dissimilar to the one in which we lived. Ironically, he had a poster of Frank Zappa seated on a toilet bowl on the back of his bathroom door - 'Phi Zappa Krappa' – it said. James said it was something left over from his college days. I never did tell him that I thought he resembled the musician, but then, I never did tell him much of anything. When he asked about my family, more out of courtesy than curiosity, I told him that I had a married sister and a niece up north, and that my parents were dead. I think I mentioned my brother in the Air Force once when we were discussing postcards. That was the extent of our personal conversations.

Our relationship may have been superficial, but it was sensual as hell. James was an expert lover, and was no doubt ruining me for any future encounters with the opposite sex. He was quiet, soft, and tender. He took his time making love, as though it were an art that he had perfected. I didn't feel like I was in love with him, but I desired him in a romantic way that would leave me unable to think about anything, except the act itself. I really didn't understand it at all. I'd had no experience, and had never even had a conversation with anyone about it. I'd always assumed that I'd fall in love, and the rest would take care of itself. But this didn't feel like love, it felt like lust.

We'd spend our days off in the park, or at the beach, each of us reading, or talking about books we'd read, or in bed. James would recommend books that he thought I'd like, and I'd recommend music to him. I had a habit of singing whatever tune was playing in my head without even thinking about it, and he'd always ask, *"What's that song you're singing?"* I think it could have been a good relationship because it was so peaceful and serene, but it wasn't meant to be.

Because Brady and I had never bothered to get a telephone, everyone contacted me by mail or through the restaurant's phone, and most of my mail went through Mr. Davis, the lawyer. One morning when I got to work there was a note up above the time clock for me reading: "Call Jayne ASAP!"

I felt the panic rise in my chest. Something had to be seriously wrong, because Jayne never considered anything an emergency. Even when she'd found out that I'd killed Marcucci, she'd taken the news in stride, saying that sooner or later somebody had to kill him, it might as well be me! Sure enough, she was calling to tell me that Charlie had died the day before of a massive coronary. Jayne offered to drive down to Asbury to pick me up, but I wouldn't let her; she had her hands full with her mom and all of the arrangements. I told her that I'd travel up there by bus.

I phoned James at the library to tell him I was going, and he offered to take a few days off and come with me. He said he'd stay with his parents, and that I could call him whenever I needed him and he'd be there in a flash. This was as demonstrative as he'd ever been, and that made me uncomfortable. I wasn't sure that I wanted him 'in' my life. He was separate and safe. Now suddenly, he was trying to invade my past, and meet people who were part of my 'other' life. I didn't think that I could deal with that, not now, anyway. I wasn't comfortable with the merging of my past and present just yet, I hadn't fully processed it all, and I was unsure of how to proceed.

I tried to put him off, saying that I didn't want to be a bother. I told him that it was just as easy for me to catch a bus up there, but he insisted and persisted. I had a dilemma, I honestly didn't want him to come with me, and yet I didn't feel comfortable telling him the truth.

Brady hadn't offered to come with me, she was happy to keep moving forward without ever looking back. There was nothing in her past that brought her any joy, and now I felt much the same. I didn't think that James would understand that, though I thought he should. He'd had a past life that didn't have anything to do with our relationship. I didn't want any part of his past, nor did I want him to have anything to do with mine. I was trying to move on, and live in the present. If James was trying to become involved in my past, then that meant that he thought there would be a future for us, and I wasn't ready for a future, it was too soon. I had to have a present first, I had to figure out who I was before I could move on with any sort of future plans.

I paced around the apartment while waiting for him to come over. He had never been to our place before, because I hadn't wanted him in my space. I'd never come out and told him that, but I'm sure he'd figured that out. Suddenly, I started to feel claustrophobic, and I couldn't breathe. I felt a sense of panic and dread rising up, like something very bad was going to happen. It seemed like a good time to recite that Serenity Prayer, and I repeated the chant in my head to calm myself. I jumped up when I heard his knock at the door, and opened it to find James standing there, tall, dark and haunted.

"What's wrong? Why are you crying?" he asked.

Oh, shit, I was doing it again. I wondered how a person could cry without realizing it, and when James moved in to embrace and comfort me, I jumped back, as though I'd been bitten.

"What's wrong, Marra? What is it?" he asked, his dark eyes searching my face for an answer as he held on tightly to both of my arms.

"I don't want you to come with me," I blurted out. I didn't mean to say it, I'd wanted to be diplomatic and kind, but there it was, out of my mouth before I'd even fully processed the thought.

I could see the shock and confusion in his eyes, and then something else, like sadness, or resignation.

"I see," he said, as he slowly released hold of my arms.

"It's just something that I have to do alone," I tried to explain, although I really didn't comprehend it myself.

"I understand," he said, "You have to do everything alone."

"What do you mean by that?" I could hear the edge in my own voice as I'd said it. I felt the anger rising up from my gut. I didn't know why I was mad, but I was.

James shook his head slowly, and turned away from me. Walking back to the door with his head hung low, he looked dejected. It pained me to see how I'd hurt him.

"I'm sorry, James, it's got nothing to do with you. Please don't take it personally," I pleaded.

I thought that he'd understand, but it was clear by his expression that he didn't. It hadn't been my intention to hurt him, I was only trying to protect myself, but I didn't know how to explain that to him.

He turned to face me and, with as much emotion as I'd ever heard in his voice said, "Marra, nothing is personal with you, is it? I get it, and I guess I've always known that it would end like this. That's why I was always careful with you, I was careful not to try and get too close. You don't want me in your space, and maybe you don't want anybody in your space, maybe it has nothing at all to do with me and everything to do with you, but it still hurts."

I saw a tear roll down his cheek just before he turned back toward the door and stepped out of my life forever. I called his name, but I'll never know whether he heard me and ignored it, or he didn't hear me at all.

Then I cried; not the silent tears that I didn't even know were there, but loud, desperate tears. I cried so loud that I had to throw myself onto my bed and bury my head into my pillow so that the whole neighborhood wouldn't hear me. I stayed there and I cried, until the crazy old lady downstairs started pounding on her ceiling with the handle of a broomstick, yelling up to me in her broken English, "Stop-a hurting dat-a baby! Stop-a dat right-a now or I'll calla da Police-a! Putana! You a no good-a putana!"

I started laughing at how ridiculous my life had become when Brady suddenly appeared in the doorway and said, "What the hell is going on here?" She stood there for a moment listening to the cacophony emanating from the lunatic below us, and then busted out laughing. We laughed until my laughter turned to tears again, and then she held me while I told her what I'd done.

CHAPTER ELEVEN

Charlie's funeral was beautiful, sad, but beautiful. If ever there was a gorgeous, grieving widow, it was Edith. Even in terrible sadness, she was the picture of poise and elegance. Jayne and I were a mess, but Edith was magnificent, running the show like a master conductor at the symphony. There were hundreds of people in attendance from all over the world; authors, poets, editors, agents, and friends. Everyone who was anyone in the literary industry knew and admired Charlie Bennison, and they'd all come to pay their final respect to a wonderful man.

Edith held court for three days; the wake, the funeral, and the more intimate gathering at their home. Jayne and I helped out when needed, but because Edith had hired a staff of people for the affair, we usually ended up out on the terrace, eating, drinking, and critiquing the characters who had come to celebrate Charlie's life. Jayne's evaluation of each person's demeanor had me in stitches. She'd conjure up entire scenarios of their life based upon their appearance and behavior. Sometimes she did have actual personal information, and had no shame in sharing the intimate details of their exploits. I hadn't laughed so hard in a very long time - and it was a great relief from the sadness for both of us.

Jayne was the city mouse to my country mouse, all made-up, and dressed like a fashion model, with a Kool menthol in one hand and a martini in the other. I dined on ginger ale and pretzels, and I preferred jeans, peasant blouses, and just a smidge of lip gloss. We were opposites, but seemed to mesh well emotionally. Jayne had a gift of taking whatever sorrow I'd be feeling, and she'd find something good about it. She'd explain to me that all of my trials were character building, and were strengthening me for some future time when I'd be called upon for greatness. The way Jayne expressed her thoughts were enough to make even *me* think that maybe there was something better coming. I envied her aplomb, never any self-doubt or apathy. Jayne was always so sure of herself.

I stayed on for the remainder of the week with Edith and Jayne, but knew it was time to split when they both began to badger me about continuing my education. I wasn't ready yet - I wasn't able to become anything yet, because first I had to become a real person, not just the shell of a girl who was hiding from her own feelings.

I headed back to Asbury Park and back to work, but I avoided the library. Brady told me that she'd seen James around town a few times looking miserable, and told me that she'd felt sorry for him.

"I thought you didn't like him?" I asked.

"Well, I never said I didn't *like* him, he just isn't my type. He's too quiet, too old, and kind of spooky!"

"He's not that old, and I like quiet," I said.

"Well, you obviously don't like it *that* much!"

I stuck my tongue out at her, and then Brady reciprocated the gesture. We giggled like a couple of kids, although I felt as though I'd never actually been a kid. I couldn't remember a time when I'd felt secure, when I didn't have to worry about something, or someone. There was always fighting in the house I grew up in, even in the middle of the night when I'd be fast asleep. I'd awaken to hear my parent's angry voices, accusing each other of ruining one another's lives. My father's drunken rants were frightening, and I'd always end up crying myself to sleep after he'd quieted down. Shelby would have her transistor radio earphones in, and a pillow over her head for extra protection. Whenever I'd try to talk to her about it the next day she'd say, "What are you talking about, Marra? I didn't hear anything!"

I had dreams about Charlie for the next solid week. The dreams were always the same; Charlie, looking dapper in a suit and tie, leaning against a piano, tapping on his watch, and looking at me. What could that mean, that I was running out of time? What good were dreams if you couldn't interpret them, and how was I supposed to figure out what Charlie was trying to tell me?

A few weeks later I had my answer, and I realized that I was in deep trouble. I hadn't been feeling well, but I put that down to the stress of Charlie's death, and my breaking up with James, or I should say, James breaking up with me. I was finishing up my shift at the restaurant late one stormy afternoon and peeked out the back door just in time to see huge, dark, storm clouds blowing in from over the ocean, when the feeling of nausea and dizziness hit me like a ton of bricks. Hank, the fry-cook, grabbed me on my way down toward the floor.

"Whoa, honey! Take it easy now," Hank said, as he led me over to a chair. "Just sit right down here, and I'll get you a glass of water."

Hank came back with a glass of water, and a cold, wet washcloth for my forehead. I sipped and breathed, then put the washcloth over my eyes for a few minutes until I started feeling better.

"You okay now, sweetie?" Hank asked.

"Yeah, thanks. I must be coming down with something, all that traveling on a bus, with sick people coughing all over me!" I feigned laughter, but I could feel the dread bubbling up from deep inside me.

Hank insisted on driving me home, even though his shift wasn't over for another three hours. I was fighting waves of nausea from one side of town to the other, while a driving hail pelted Hank's GTO convertible top, threatening to tear through the vinyl at any moment. Hank probably believed that my pale-faced fear was a side effect of the scary weather, but precipitation had nothing to do with the source of my fear. Hank offered to see me in, but I wouldn't hear of it, especially in light of the treacherous weather.

I went inside, dried off and lay down on the bed, full of dread, knowing what my problem was. I hadn't had a period in six weeks, and I knew what that meant. How could I have been so stupid? How could I have let this happen? I cried miserably, until sleep finally overtook me.

When Brady came home, she woke me up to see how I was feeling. Hank had told her that I'd almost passed out, and that he'd taken me home early, and it didn't take Brady long to put two and two together.

"You're pregnant, aren't you?" she asked.

"Oh, Brady, how could I be so stupid? What am I going to do?" I cried.

Brady held me until I had no tears left, and then we discussed every aspect and possibility. Brady asked me what I *wanted* to do.

"Well, I certainly can't have a child, not in my current situation. I can't imagine having one and giving it up for adoption, although that's what I've always thought I would do in this situation. And even if I do have it . . . if James ever found out, he'd never let me put it up for adoption, not after losing his other two kids."

I felt as though I was in a dark place, from which there seemed no escape. A child means a future, and I didn't have the luxury of a future yet, I was having enough trouble with the present. I was certainly not capable of being a parent, or of being anything, really. I was having trouble just being me, whoever I was.

"What should I do Brady?" I implored her.

"Oh, honey, you know that I can't tell you that. If I had a crystal ball and I could see into the future, then maybe I could help you with this, but I don't, and I can't."

"What would you do?" I asked her.

"I have absolutely no idea. I'd be just as confused and scared as you are. I'm sorry, sweetie."

Brady looked as miserable as I felt. She really understood what I was feeling, and commiserated with me while we made list after list of the pros and cons of each option. Then Brady said that she believed that I needed to take a few days to rest, so that I'd have a clearer head with which to make a decision.

I spent the entire weekend in bed, sick as a dog. I'm sure it was psychological, due to the stress of the situation. Finally, under great duress, a decision was made, and I got an appointment with the Monmouth County Women's Clinic. Brady came with me, held my hand, and told me not to worry; it would all be over soon. But some things are never over, the memories of them live somewhere inside of your consciousness and rise up to haunt you when you least expect them.

The experience was dreadful, painful, and humiliating. The clinic workers were true to their moniker, they were clinical, unfeeling, and unsympathetic. The procedure was painful, not merely 'uncomfortable' as they'd said it would be. When it was over, I felt empty in every sense of the word, and worse than the emptiness was the guilt I felt. I could tell myself a million different things, and fill my own thoughts with platitudes, but it couldn't change the truth of what my heart knew – there had been a baby, and I'd killed it. I'd discarded its life and its future like yesterday's trash. I didn't think that I could go on living with that knowledge, knowing that I'd done the most despicable thing that a human being can do. I'd taken an innocent life.

When I left the Procedure Room, instructions in hand, I was light-headed and wobbly, and probably would have fallen if not for Brady's arm holding me upright. We had to pass through the waiting room on the way out, and while I tried not to make eye-contact with any of the women there, I couldn't help but notice Donna, Dino's wife, looking right at me, with the strangest expression on her face.

Part of my brain said, *'Stop her! Tell her not to do it'*, yet I knew that wasn't realistic. I couldn't do that to a waiting room full of girls and women who had already spent enough time agonizing over a no-win decision that would alter their lives forever. Besides, who was I to tell anyone else what to do with their own life? I was the princess of poor choices. I was a twenty-one-year-old whose life was already in the toilet. The picture of Frank Zappa from the poster on the door in James's apartment flashed in my mind's eye, representing yet another personal failure.

I ran a fever for days after my procedure, and Brady stayed by my side, feeding me soup, ice water, and antibiotics. I was more than just depressed, I was despondent. My dreams were filled with bloody babies, screaming for help. I woke up remembering the old lady downstairs yelling, *"Stop-a hurting dat-a baby! Stop-a dat right-a now or I'll calla da Police-a! Putana! You a no good-a putana!"* That was the day that James had walked out of my life. The old lady's rant had been an omen, she was foretelling my future; but I hadn't heeded her warning, I'd only laughed at the foolish old woman who had heard my cries and thought it was a baby.

I wore my pain and guilt like a shroud, even when I was back on my feet again. I had gotten painfully thin, and everyone who saw me asked how I was feeling. They'd known I'd been ill, but not why, and I certainly wasn't going to share that with anyone. Only Brady and Donna knew the truth, but Donna had moved out the following month after announcing that she was divorcing Dino. She and I had never made eye contact again after that moment in the Clinic's waiting room, because I couldn't bear to look at her. Brady kept encouraging me to get counseling, but I refused. I couldn't speak about my guilt and pain, it would've hurt too much.

I also couldn't bear to see babies or small children. I really didn't want to see anyone, but eventually I had to go back to work. Mercifully, I was in the kitchen most of the time, and didn't have to deal with patrons and their children, but there were times I'd hear a little one cry and it would tear at my heartstrings. Brady kept telling me that I needed to get over it, and I'd glare at her. I thought that she should have known better, she'd taken a life; she knew you never, ever get over it. The great irony of my life was, after I had justifiably killed someone I was punished, locked up for two and a half years; but when I took an innocent life, there was no punishment, just a prescription and bed rest. I could walk the streets, free as a bird, after killing a baby - and so I began walking. I didn't eat or sleep, I just kept walking.

I walked the length of the Boardwalk, rain or shine, around the Carousel, around Sunset Lake, over to Ocean Grove, and then back again. I'd walk to Deal, and then back to Asbury, and then walk over to Ocean Grove, and back again. I walked until I couldn't walk any more, until I collapsed in the street on Kingsley Avenue, and woke up in the Monmouth Medical Center emergency room with Brady standing over me.

"Are you done yet, Marra?" Brady said, with tears spilling down her cheeks. "Are you finished trying to kill yourself? You need to get help, Marra! You need to find a way to put this behind you, and go on with your life!"

Brady was angry, and I couldn't blame her. She didn't need my grief, she'd had enough of her own. Brady was trying to get on with her life, while I was dragging her back into the quagmire of my despair. I knew that I had to get away from this place, because the memories it held for me were killing my spirit. If I had any chance at all of surviving I had to find a new place to live. It was time for me to move on.

"Yes, Brady," I said, "I'm done with it."

PART III

1981, Age 27

Running On Empty

I-95 South is a drag to drive, even with my *Who's Next* tape blaring. I got bored and switched on the radio, but they were playing songs that reminded me of things I didn't want to think about; *Stairway to Heaven*, *Don't Fear the Reaper*, and *Knockin' on Heaven's Door*. I switched back to the Who tape.

My crappy sunglasses weren't doing much to cut the road glare, and although the AC in my new, black Toyota Cressida was cranked, I still felt the sun's heat baking my left arm. There was nothing to see on this stretch of road, and I wasn't sure I-4 West would be much better once I reached it.

I was running from death once again, it seemed to follow me like a shadow on a sunny day. It seemed to be my fate in life to constantly be in the valley of the shadow of death, but I *did* fear evil. I didn't know if it would be any better where I was going than it was from where I'd come, but I hoped it would.

I knew that some believed that we are masters of our own destiny. I was not of that school of thought. I imagined myself a ladybug on a leaf in the river, floating where the river flows, holding on for dear life, until the winds let up, and I fly back to shore and discover what God has for me there. Once I'd found what I was looking for, I'd resume my trek downstream to the next river bank, and the next after that, until, eventually, I'm in the open sea.

CHAPTER TWELVE

Six years earlier . . .

I spent my first four years in Charleston taking care of my grandfather, Papa Joe. He was delighted to have me come and stay with him, as he was in dire need of help. He was seventy-nine-years-old and had needed a hip replacement for ten years, but his heart wouldn't hold up to the surgery. It took me six weeks to get him to use a cane, the stubborn old buzzard. I could see who Mama had taken after, that's for sure.

He was a typical curmudgeon, always finding fault with everything and everyone - and you'd think he was the only normal, genuine American, by the way he labeled every person by size, color, nationality, religion, or sexual orientation. He'd never admit that he was hard of hearing; he just assumed that nobody else could hear something if he couldn't, and so he never lowered his voice when commenting on *'the size of that colored woman's bee-hind'* or *'the honker on that Jewish fella'*. It was exasperating to try and explain to him just *why* his comments were totally inappropriate. He'd just say that I was out of touch with reality, and call me a new-fangled communist. His house was falling apart, but he'd insist that he couldn't afford to fix anything. I happened to know that he had more money than Rockefeller stashed away for a rainy day.

"Papa Joe, this is the rainy day! You're roof is leaking and it's going to blow clean off with the next storm, unless you have it replaced now!" I'd implore him, but his response was always the same.

"Miss Marra, these Charleston roofers are maggots! They steal your hard-earned cash, and run 'way without doin' the job y'all paid 'em fah'."

Everyone you had to pay was a 'maggot', according to Papa Joe. He was tighter than a tick up a crab's ass. His neighbors stayed clear of him, and the shop owners gave him a wide berth when he entered their stores. I imagine that everyone in Charleston had had a run in with him at one time or another.

But, God bless him, he never once brought up my past. He never asked me what had happened, where I'd been, or mentioned anything about Mama's death. The only time he mentioned Mama's name was when he'd tell stories from when she was a little girl. Once in a while he'd slip, and call me Charlotte Eve. I'm not sure if he was really all there, but when it came time to count his money, he was as sharp as a tack.

My grandfather didn't believe in socializing at any level, he kept to himself, and expected everyone else to do the same. He'd warn me not to get taken in by 'so-called' friendly neighbors. He'd tell me that they really weren't being friendly; they were just trying to extract information. Every time I'd be headed outside he'd say, "Watch your step 'round the neighborhood news-hounds! Loose lips sink ships!"

I'd had a few people in the neighborhood approach me early on, but I wasn't inclined to share much, and kept to myself. I'm sure neighbors thought I was anti-social because I was Old Man Whitford's granddaughter, but I'd had my own reasons. I didn't want anyone to know about my past. There were times that I'd be tempted to strike up a conversation with the nice old lady next door, or the young mother who walked by with the stroller every afternoon, but I'd been afraid to. Only having my grandfather to talk to was exasperating, as conversation was *not* his strong suit. Papa Joe's personality was much more disagreeable outside the house than it was inside; there were times that he was downright sweet. Well, maybe that's stretching it a bit, but he was generally nice to *me*.

I'm sure Papa Joe appreciated my help, but I don't remember him ever thanking me for anything. The first Father's Day I was with him I'd decided that I'd take his old, worn rocker from the front porch, and give it a fresh coat of paint. I thought about buying him a new one, but I knew that I'd get a lecture about wasting money on needless enterprises. I'd been so proud of myself, I'd done a beautiful job, and the old rocker looked practically new. As soon as it was dry I set it on the front porch with a big, red bow on it, and called Papa Joe out to look. He stared at it for a few moments, and then scratched his head. Peering up at me through his wrinkly, old, squinted eyes, he said, "Ya' know, Miss Marra, you ken cover a thang up, but that don't make it a differn't thang. It jus' is what it is," and he turned around and went back inside, and plopped his old self down in the big, overstuffed, floral chair that sat three feet from the big, color console television set with the rabbit ears. I'm sure I was standing there with my mouth hanging open for a bit. I never could figure out half of what my grandfather was talking about until after his death, when secrets were revealed.

I dreamed about Mama often while I lived in her childhood home. In one dream, I stood over her as she was rocking in the rocker I'd painted, and she was smiling up at me. At first, I thought she was trying to tell me what a good job I'd done refurbishing the chair, but when I looked at her again, she was holding a baby in her arms, and they were both smiling up at me. I knew that it was my baby, and that Mama was letting me know that she was taking good care of her. I woke up with tears streaming down my cheeks, and a sense of peace I hadn't felt before. If Mama and my baby were somewhere together, then maybe I could move on with my life.

In another dream, Mama was walking up stairs, and beckoning me to follow her, but the only stairs in this house went up to the attic. When I inquired what might be up there, Papa Joe insisted that there was nothing but spiders, so Mama would have to go up there without me, I don't cotton to spiders. Mama seemed happy in my dreams, as if she were glad to be back at home, and so I was happy for her. Maybe she'd finally rest in peace, and maybe all we had been through would finally be worth something of value.

After a few months, I knew it was high time for me to start doing something more constructive with my life than just cooking, cleaning, and sitting around watching my grandfather snooze all day. When I realized that I could easily get in to the College of Charleston, I called Tom Davis, the Judge's lawyer, and told him that I was ready to tap into my college fund. The trust had grown with interest, and there was enough money in it for me to pursue my master's degree. Mr. Davis advised me that he'd help me expedite the process, but there was a pressing matter we needed to discuss. The Judge's nephew was preparing a court battle to contest my having been named as a beneficiary of his uncle's will. I told Mr. Davis to let the Judge's nephew know that I would release my claim on the estate, if he would send me the Judge's chess set. Mr. Davis, being a lawyer, strongly advised against that. He said that I could be forfeiting millions of dollars, and said how foolish I would be to give that up without a fight. But I didn't care about the Judge's money, it wasn't rightfully mine anyway. I wasn't a blood relative, just a girl upon whom the Judge had taken pity. The Judge had given me more than I deserved already, and all I wanted was something of his that held good memories for me; I had so few of them in my life.

Naturally, the Judge's nephew jumped at my offer, and the gift-wrapped chess set arrived in Charleston with a thank-you card containing a generous check. Papa Joe and I spent many an afternoon out on the front porch playing chess for matchsticks, as they were the only form of currency that my grandfather could bear to part with. Those were the times that I remember my grandfather being the happiest; and the larger his pile of matchsticks, the happier he would be.

I got the occasional call from Jayne, who was engaged to be married to a wealthy young lawyer from Boston named Dylan Fitzpatrick. Edith was delighted, and was keeping herself busy planning a lavish wedding for the following summer.

Brady sent a letter saying she'd dumped Freddie for the bass player in his band, a 'stud' named Raymond. For some reason, I just couldn't picture it. It seemed to me that anyone named Raymond couldn't possibly be stud-like, but there it was. Brady's news was short and sweet, and other than her new beau, she'd given no clue as to what else was going on in her life.

Will still sent his postcards, and my grandfather had become as enamored with them as Mama had been. He'd hung them all on the kitchen wall, like some ridiculous, white trash, pop-art display. Every so often I'd find Papa Joe bent over, eyes squinted, mouth agape, studying one of them with his magnifying glass, as if it held some secret of the universe. He'd look up at me, eyes wide, and say, "You know what, Miss Marra, I think I'll visit this place someday."

I didn't have the heart to say what I knew was the truth – that he'd never spend a nickel to visit *any* place, so I'd just replied, "Sounds good, Papa Joe!"

CHAPTER THIRTEEN

I met John Lloyd Maybank, whose ancestors had been Charleston gentry for generations, while walking to school one day. He sat smugly on the front porch of one of his family's antebellum estates, and whistled at me as if I were a dog. I shot him a nasty expression, and hurried my step.

Moments later, I heard someone walking behind me, and then felt his breath in my hair, as he softly whistled *Dixie*. Rather than let the lout intimidate me, I stopped and turned quickly, causing him to stumble backwards and fall on his backside on a freshly-mowed lawn, right into a pink hibiscus bush. I laughed at the horrified expression on his face, and then he began to laugh as well. I saw then that he was the most beautiful man I'd ever set eyes on, almost too good to be true.

"I do declay-ah, Miss Scah-lett," he said, reaching his hand up to me, "I fear that I have found myself in a very precarious situation. Would ya'll mind givin' an ol' boy a hand?"

I reached out to him, and grabbed his outstretched hand. Pulling with all my might, I struggled to haul him up, only to have him pull me down, right into his lap.

"Y'all 'er not as strong as I would've suspected by that surly expression on y'alls bee-u-ti-ful face!" he drawled, his gorgeousness just inches from my face.

I burst out laughing at the total absurdity of it all. Here I was, sitting in the lap of a total stranger, on a busy Charleston street, in the middle of the day, with passersby gawking. The mustachioed homeowner on whose lawn we sat came out onto his front porch to see what the commotion was about, and stared down at the two of us incredulously. I pushed the handsome stranger (in whose lap I was perched) down, and popped up before he could grab onto me again.

I addressed him in my best southern drawl, "Sir, I do believe that it is *way* too early in the day for a gentleman as youthful as yourself to begin drinkin'. I do believe that you have a *prob*-lem, and that you should check your sorry ass into the local Alcoholics Anonymous meetin', just as soon as you can pick it up off of this po' man's front lawn."

As I turned and scurried down the street, I heard his raucous laughter bellowing behind me. He caught up with me just as I was about to enter the school library, placing his large hand over my small one, just as I grasped the door handle. He introduced himself properly, after apologizing profusely for accosting me in broad daylight. He was so *very* handsome and charming, that I found myself being sucked into his schmooze.

Now here was a guy I could fall for; tall, with sandy, sun-streaked hair, and sparkling, robin's-egg-blue eyes. His dimples deepened when he smiled, and his teeth were brilliantly white and even. His body was lean and muscled, but not overly so. I felt, for the first time in my young life, that I was under the spell of another human being. He was enchanting, and I found myself grinning from ear to ear, as I offered my hand to introduce myself. He gently pressed his full lips to the backs of my fingers, and those gorgeous eyes peeked up at me. All I could think was, what luck!

But *my* luck, as it were, held true to form. The great love affair that I could have easily imagined with this southern hunk was not to be. John Lloyd was destined to love me, just as he did in my dream world, but unfortunately, only as a friend. His reluctance at romance was no reflection on my womanhood because, as I'd eventually come to realize, *his* preference was not for *any* woman. It took me some time to figure that out, though, because he was not forthcoming with this very critical information. I don't think that he was trying to be evasive about who he was, I just don't think he was totally confident about it back then. Homosexuality was not generally accepted by the old southern guard, so John Lloyd was happy to have me on his arm at the many public and family functions we'd attend in order to keep up proper appearances. I loved the man and I was, perhaps, a bit delusional about our future together.

The Maybanks were one of the wealthiest families in Charleston. John Lloyd's daddy, H.B. Maybank, grandson of both Hugh J. Barrett, and John Maybank, owned properties in and around Charleston, including some islands off the Carolina coast that he had developed, or was in the process of developing. H.B. was unhappy that John Lloyd hadn't followed him into that aspect of the family business. Instead, he had chosen a Fine Arts degree from the College of Charleston, and would take over his Aunt Luanne's business, Maybank Fine Art and Antiques on King Street. John Lloyd's mother, Annabelle Beatrice Lloyd, a direct descendant of the family who owned Lloyd's of London, came from an international insurance dynasty. John Lloyd Maybank was Charleston royalty, as were the generations of his family who had preceded him.

After John Lloyd and I had become very close, he confided in me, albeit in an opaque way, about his sexual orientation. I convinced him to experiment romantically a bit, after I insisted that perhaps he'd been deluded by some misguided infatuation. I insisted that he kiss me, although he assured me that he had done much more than just kiss girls before, and hadn't enjoyed it the way a young man should. I'd found that impossible to believe, and thought that it was only because he hadn't been with the *right* girl (me!). In my heart, I was hoping to bring him back into the fold, and believed that if he truly loved me, it would all work out. I had to be absolutely certain before I gave up on the idea of a real romance with him, the man of my dreams.

His kisses were delicious, soft and tender, and they'd made me melt. But I knew in my heart that there wasn't any real romantic passion on his part. Sadly, I had to conclude that there was no point in trying to push a real relationship with him any further. We'd kiss in public, so that his persona would remain intact, but that was the extent of our physical relationship, besides brotherly hugs and friendly hand-holding. That aside, I was delighted to have his friendship and love. He made me feel special, and merely being in his presence gave me a sense of security that I'd never felt before.

The Maybank family seemed genuinely delighted with our faux-courtship, which led me to believe that they weren't totally in the dark about John Lloyd's proclivity toward his own gender. He was especially affectionate to me in front of family members; there was a lot of hand-holding, hugging, kissing, and the occasional ass-grab. I have to admit that I enjoyed every bit of it, faux or not. He was totally perfect for me in every way, with that one exception – but boy, was it ever a doozy!

At his sister's wedding, John Lloyd had been asked to sing, delighting the crowd with his soulful, magnificent voice. Whether he sang Bob Dylan, the Beatles, or James Taylor, he'd nail it every time; you'd swear you were listening to the original artist. He and I would often sing duets, and while my own voice was pretty good, I couldn't hold a candle to John Lloyd. As he took the stage and performed Minnie Riperton's hit, *Lovin' You*, he gazed into my eyes, causing me to briefly forget that our romance was not an authentic one. Returning to my side, he held me in an embrace and nuzzled my neck, as his mother swooned behind us.

I'd always known that Annabelle never cared for me, but had merely tolerated my presence for John Lloyd's sake. For her, our faux courtship had the added benefit of completing her fantasy of John Lloyd as the masculine heir to the family's fortune. I'd overheard Annabelle casually mentioning John Lloyd's and my future offspring in countless conversations with her pretentious society matrons. According to Annabelle, John Lloyd and I were planning on having a *very* large family, indeed! When I'd appeared at the bridesmaid's luncheon where she was holding court, and spouting that exact fabrication, I thought she'd change the subject, or look embarrassed when she realized that I'd heard her. Instead, she'd said, "Isn't that right, Miss Marra?"

Without missing a beat, I'd responded, "Mother always knows best, Miss Annabelle!" And I'd smiled at the group of women like the obedient, fraudulent debutant I was.

A few months later, at Jayne's wedding, John Lloyd and I performed *Lovin' You* as a duet. Everyone there had been charmed by John Lloyd's southern accent, charisma, and phenomenally handsome good looks. I always felt like a princess on his arm, and knew that I was the envy of every single woman around, and even a few married ones. If they'd only known the truth! Afterward, when we were alone, I told him how much he meant to me, and how I wished that the love song we'd sung to each other was the truth. He held me close and said, "But it is the truth, darlin'. I more than love you, Marra Dallas, I adore you."

John Lloyd insisted that he loved me in a way that surpassed mere physical love, that he loved me with his very soul. He told me that he thought we might have been twins in another lifetime, two halves of a whole. I loved him, and I trusted him more than I'd ever trusted anyone. John Lloyd didn't expect anything from me, except my friendship. He was nurturing, and protective of me, and that gave me a sense of security. But honestly, I still fantasized of a romance with him.

John Lloyd's family grasped the fantasy of our courtship with relish. They chose to believe that he was a healthy, heterosexual, all-American boy. And while his family was thrilled about our close relationship, my grandfather, on the other hand, was less than delighted.

Mr. Joseph Drayton Whitford wasn't particularly enamored with anyone in Charleston as far as I could see, but he especially despised the Maybank family. He didn't care to elaborate on the subject, but he'd made it quite clear to me that I had chosen the worst possible gentleman in all of Charleston to befriend.

I tried as best I could to explain to Papa Joe that John Lloyd Maybank and I were just friends, and would never, ever, be anything more than that, but that didn't make one bit of difference to him. I even entertained the idea of explaining to him *exactly* why he needn't worry about my relationship with John Lloyd, but knowing Papa Joe, that would've just opened another can of worms. I wouldn't give up the only friend I'd had since leaving New Jersey almost a year before, so I managed to keep the two of them out of spitting distance for the next three and a half years.

In the end, my grandfather came around when he saw John Lloyd's kindness and tenderness, both to me, and to himself, as his health declined. In his last months, when he'd been too frail to walk, Papa Joe allowed John Lloyd to carry him, rather than submit to the wheelchair I'd foolishly rented for him. He'd allowed John Lloyd to help him bathe and dress, as it wasn't proper for a girl to care for the personal needs of an old man, according to Papa Joe. I would never have been able to give my grandfather the care he needed without John Lloyd's constant help. He'd practically moved in with us at the end, in case I needed him during the night. It was then I started calling him *'my angel'*, causing his blush to rise, his dimples to deepen, and his baby blues to sparkle. God, how I loved that man.

In those four years I'd lived with him, I'd come to love my grandfather as much as I'd ever loved anyone, and that made his passing all the more difficult for me. John Lloyd adeptly handled all of the arrangements after my grandfather died, including a church service. Papa Joe would have spit daggers to know that his body was being prayed over in a church, as he'd believed that organized religion was just a sham to steal your hard-earned cash. The catered luncheon afterward, in a private room at the swanky Le Bordeaux, would have had him spinning in his grave at the expense alone! His disdain for opulence had only been surpassed by his hatred for those who lavished themselves with it.

All of the Maybank family had been in attendance, as were various neighbors and Papa Joe's attorney, who, besides me and John Lloyd, seemed to be the only one there who'd ever had any sort of genuine and cordial relationship with my grandfather. Shelby couldn't come because she was eight months pregnant with her second child, and Will was out of the country and couldn't make it home in time. There didn't seem to be anyone else to contact. Considering that Papa Joe had spent a lifetime shunning the company of others, I was pleased that there were so many warm bodies in attendance. I so appreciated John Lloyd's efforts to give my grandfather a memorable sendoff, even if Papa Joe would have found it all an ostentatious display of hedonistic affluence. Of course, that's not what he would have called it. He would have just called it a party of money-grubbing maggots!

After the affair was over, my grandfather's attorney came back to the house to discuss Papa Joe's last will and testament. My grandfather had left a few thousand dollars each to Shelby and Will, and everything else to me. He was worth quite a bit, maybe not the millions that the Judge had been worth, but much more than anyone would have guessed judging by his standard of living.

CHAPTER FOURTEEN

I spent the next two years finishing up my degree and hanging out with John Lloyd. He helped me study, taught me how to cook seafood, and he taught me how to drive – and I nearly destroyed his BMW in the process. John Lloyd and I had become inseparable over time, and while he had shared his greatest secrets with me, I was still withholding mine from him. He knew that I was guarding my secrets and was patient with me, but after Papa Joe's death, he told me that it was time to come clean. I never would have believed that I could be capable of opening myself up to anyone, but I felt safe with John Lloyd. That first night after the funeral we sat up talking into the wee hours of the morning, and I confessed to him everything that had happened in my life up to that point, sobbing throughout my story of heartache, violence, and death.

I was anxious throughout my monologue that John Lloyd would be appalled by the things I'd done, and leave me in disgust and revulsion. Instead, he was tender and understanding. He talked to me about the God he knew, and his God was one of unconditional love. John Lloyd's God already knew who we were, what we'd done, said, and thought, and loved us just the same. He explained that there is not one of us who is without sin, and that there is no sin that is unforgivable. John Lloyd seemed so certain, so sure of himself, and I knew there and then that I wanted to believe in that same God, the way he believed. But I couldn't truly say whether or not that God existed in this dark and dismal world. Then, after he'd shared his faith, John Lloyd Maybank held me close and sang *Bridge Over Troubled Water* until I was fast asleep.

My confessions had lifted a heavy burden from my heart and bonded me even closer to my beautiful, loving angel. I woke the next day feeling lighter and ready to do the work that lay ahead of me, the challenge of tackling the mess that was Papa Joe's house.

John Lloyd, always my faithful companion, helped me clear out my grandfather's house to ready it for sale. It was during the house cleaning process that I found the life changing secrets that had been buried for decades up in Papa Joe's attic. I finally realized what Mama had been trying to tell me in my dreams when encouraging me to go up those attic steps.

One afternoon, while separating all of Papa Joe's crap into piles, John Lloyd suggested we go up and begin to tackle the shambles that awaited us up in the attic. I was amazed, never had I seen so much junk stored in one small place in my life. There was dust and cobwebs everywhere, suggesting that the space had been undisturbed for several decades.

"This is ridiculous! I say we leave it alone, and sell the place 'as is'!" I protested, while spitting out the spider's silken strings.

"Now darlin', we've got to get through this, so y'all may as well quit your cussin' and fussin', and start carryin' these treasures downstairs. Besides, darlin', we might just strike gold up here," he laughed. Holding up an old brass candlestick and thrusting it in my general direction as if he were fencing, he yelled, "En garde!"

"And what do you call that maneuver, prep-school fencing boy?" I asked, laughing at his ridiculous stance.

"Passado!"

"Well, passado to you too, cowboy, now would you stop playing musketeer so that we can get the hell out of this dump!"

"Darlin', y'all gotta have more fun in life, the journey's gotta be part of the adventure!" He admonished me, while grinning like a loon. John Lloyd's joy of living was contagious, and made the chores at hand bearable.

Our first viable attic 'discovery' was an old cedar chest, filled with my mother's things. I was delighted by this find. It contained Mama's old baby dolls, clothing, and even a pressed corsage that was hidden between the pages of a diary – a diary! I convinced John Lloyd to help me maneuver the chest down the narrow stairwell so that we could go through it later, at our leisure. We spent the entire day up in that attic, filling two boxes of lawn and leaf bags with garbage. There were a few items that looked promising, according to John Lloyd - an old Morris chair that might be a Stickley, an old portrait by Jeremiah Theus, whoever he was, and a family Bible, that was worth at least sentimental value, if nothing else. Most of the rest of it was trash.

John Lloyd insisted that he'd clean up the valuable stuff and take it to his shop. He'd have a friend of his who specialized in art and antique furnishings take a look at it all. I assumed that this fellow was one of his 'special' friends. John Lloyd would talk to me about pretty much everything, and I know he would have told me more about his friend, but I'd made it clear to him that I didn't want to know about his sex life, and didn't want to share mine either. Of course, during that time, I didn't have a sex life, but that was beside the point.

I'd had more than my share of interested young men approach me over the years I spent in Charleston, but I'd always rebuff them by saying that I had a boyfriend. Well, I did indeed have a boyfriend; unfortunately, my boyfriend also had a boyfriend.

It wasn't until two days after we'd found it that we sat down to go through my mother's cedar chest. I pulled items out one by one, holding them up for inspection, and delighting in each thing: her high school cheerleader's uniform, a picture of a man in a sailboat, drawn by her when she was just five-years-old, and her diary, which was stuffed with all kinds of things, including an aged, yellow corsage.

Upon closer inspection, I discovered two birth certificates that had been issued by the State of South Carolina. One of them was my mother's, who was born in 1930. I sat there and figured out that she'd only been thirty-nine when she died, much too young for a life to end. It had never occurred to me that my mother was such a young woman, you never think about those things when you're a child - you think of your mother as old, though the truth was that my mother had never gotten old.

The other birth certificate was my brother Will's, and there were a couple of surprises there; one, he'd been born in South Carolina, and the other, the biggie, was that he'd been born William Barrett Whitford, and his father was listed as Hugh Barrett Maybank.

"Holy shit!" Was all that I could manage to say, as the realization dawned on me that my brother Will was also John Lloyd's brother. Rather than explain, I handed him the document. John Lloyd studied it for a few minutes, looked up at me quizzically, and then back at the document again. Earnest blue eyes probing, he asked, "This is your brother's?"

I nodded.

"He's my father's son?"

"That would appear to be the case."

"So, he was born the same year that my parents got married," he stated.

"I suppose that would explain why your father didn't marry my mother, who, by the way, was carrying his child."

My statement was delivered more sarcastically than I'd intended, and from the expression on John Lloyd's face, you'd have thought that I'd slapped him. I smiled weakly to show remorse.

"So, *your* brother is *my* brother. That's incredible! We're related, good thing we never . . . I wonder if my dad knew about this," he pondered, and then asked, "does your brother know?"

I was sure that my brother didn't know, and I had to wonder what John Lloyd had meant by *'good thing we never'* - good thing we never what? Made love? Got married? Had children together? Were these ever actually options? Would I have gone along with a charade for his family's sake and married him? Probably.

I had to call Shelby in order to get Will's current phone number, and run the gauntlet of questions about why I wanted to contact him. I simply told her that I'd found his birth certificate and wanted to send it to him.

"He's already got one," she said, "So, I suppose you figured it out then, huh?"

"You knew?" I asked incredulously. "When did you find out?"

"I heard Will and Mama fighting, and I listened. He was really mad at her for not telling him that Daddy wasn't his real father. That was right before he took off and joined the Air Force. Poor Mama was so upset."

"Did you ever talk to her about it?" I asked.

"No, I never let on that I knew. She seemed so hurt by it all, I thought it was better to just keep her secret and leave it alone."

Typical Shelby, she looked like Daddy, but she was all Mama; keeping secrets and telling lies were part and parcel of their life strategy. She'd never talked to Will about it, and from her tone, I could tell that she really didn't want to discuss it with me either. I inquired about the kids, then told her to give them my love and let her get off the phone so that she didn't have to talk about anything of any substance. Once again, good old Marra was keeping the peace, not rocking the boat.

Will seemed happy to hear from me, and he apologized for not coming to Papa Joe's funeral. He didn't seem surprised that I'd found out the truth about his paternity, and said he'd known for years that Bill Dunne wasn't his father and figured that we'd all known it too. I suppose that he'd forgotten that we'd been raised by a woman who would have made a great secret agent.

Will explained to me that he had needed his birth certificate in order to get his driver's license when he turned seventeen, and when Mama tried to put him off, he knew something was fishy. He badgered her for months, without any success. She kept putting him off, and kept making up one excuse after another. Once she realized that he wasn't going to give up, she sat him down to *'explain a few things'* before she handed the document over to him.

"Her story was that when she was sixteen, she fell in love with a boy from a family that her daddy hated. His family didn't approve of her, and had chosen someone they'd considered more *suitable* for their son to marry. When she realized that she was pregnant, she confided in the boy who had always had a crush on her, Bill Dunne. Bill suggested that they run away together, and that's what they did. She never did tell me who the boy was, though," my brother explained.

"Wait," I said to my brother, realizing that there was a huge missing piece to the story he'd been told, "she told you that she and Daddy ran away to get married, and that you were born in New Jersey?"

"Yep, that's what she said."

"But Will, that's impossible! Your birth certificate says you were born here, in South Carolina, to Charlotte Eveann Whitford and Hugh Barrett Maybank."

"Whoa, what? What are you talking about Marra? I've got a New Jersey birth certificate."

"Will, I'm looking at your birth certificate! You were born here, in South Carolina!"

The only thing we could speculate, is that when Daddy had adopted Will, they were issued a new birth certificate from the State of New Jersey. Daddy had been named as Will's 'adoptive father'. Will had no idea that he'd been born in South Carolina, or who his real father was. Will and Shelby had only known part of the story, that Bill Dunne was *not* Will's biological father; they'd had no clue as to who his real father was.

Will was incredulous when I told him that I was familiar with H.B. Maybank, his biological father, and that his brother was a close friend of mine. I told Will to hold on for a minute, and then handed the phone to John Lloyd, who, despite having been in shock himself just a short while earlier, seemed delighted to speak to his older brother.

John Lloyd very kindly tried to put Will at ease, when I knew it had to be a difficult conversation for him as well. They spoke at length, John Lloyd answering Will's questions as best he could. The last thing I heard John Lloyd say to him before hanging up the phone was, "I'm looking forward to meeting you, brother."

John Lloyd suggested that we read through the diary to see if Mama had left any more clues behind. Sure enough, there it was in black and white; Mama had been in love with a boy who was engaged to be married to someone else, someone whom his family had deemed *'more appropriate for a person of his standing'*. She didn't mention in the pages of her diary if she'd told the boy that she was pregnant with his child – she only wrote that she'd refused to tell her parents who the daddy was.

Reading the diary, we gleaned that Mama had met Bill Dunne at the St. Agnes Home for Girls, where her parents had sent her to have her baby. All the while, they'd pretended to their friends and neighbors that she'd gone up north to visit relatives. Bill had been hired by his aunt, who was the head nun at St. Agnes. Sister Marie had given Bill a job as the gardener, maintenance man, and security guard. Mama had gone to the home with the intention of giving her baby up for adoption, but changed her mind when she saw the little boy. Her parents were livid, they'd kept up appearances all those months, and there was no way they could let her move back home with a bastard child in 1946 - it would have been scandalous. They were even more appalled when they saw the baby boy, a duplicate of his daddy, H.B. Maybank.

Fortunately for Mama and her parents, Bill Dunne had fallen for the beautiful, green-eyed brunette, and promised to take her away to start a new life.

Mama's last entry in her diary read: *'Dear Diary, It's time to bid you adieu as I head off into a new life with this good man who has vowed to marry me. I will never have the life I'd dreamed of with the only man I will ever truly love, but at least I will have his child. Mama and Papa Joe both cried when they saw my baby, a picture of his daddy, whom he will never know. I know that they will keep my secret, as it is also their own. I pray that H.B. will someday realize the pain he has caused me by choosing his family over our love. I will try to be a good wife to Bill Dunne, although I will never truly love him.'*

I looked up into John Lloyd's eyes, now familiar to me as identical to those of my brother Will. They shared the same hair color, the same straight, white teeth, and the same nose in profile. Only the shapes of their faces were different, Will's being more oval, like Mama's, and John Lloyd's being rounder, like Annabelle's. Yes, it was obvious to me now that these two were brothers; both men's faces the reflection of their father, H.B. Maybank. It was then that I told John Lloyd about how Mama had come to me in my dream, and beckoned me to go up those attic stairs.

"She wanted me to find out the truth, she wanted me to know," I tearfully told him.

"Marra Dallas, if your Mama can come to you in your dreams," John Lloyd said, while hugging me close to himself, "when I die, I'm gonna' come to you in y'alls dreams and sing you to sleep every night!"

"Please, not every night! I might have company, you know?" I laughed, and hugged him tighter.

"Okay then, darlin', only whenever y'all need me."

I read the diary in its entirety, and discovered that the old, white wicker rocker out on Papa Joe's front porch, the one that I had painted for him that first Father's Day I'd been here, had been a Father's Day present to him from Mama in the first place. Perhaps he'd thought that I'd known that, and that there'd been some sort of significance in my refurbishing it for him. But I'd had no idea until I'd read that diary just what that rocker had represented in Papa Joe's mind. It had merely been a coincidence, if, in fact, there are such things in life.

CHAPTER FIFTEEN

John Lloyd and I decided that we'd meet with H.B. together to break the news that we'd discovered. I would bring Will's birth certificate and Mama's diary as proof, just in case he tried to deny it, or didn't believe us. John Lloyd was the more shaken of the two of us by this revelation. Mama had been gone for years, and I felt as though I'd never really known very much about her at all. John Lloyd, on the other hand, had believed that his family's history was public knowledge and had been for centuries. He couldn't imagine what this would do to his family. He didn't know how H.B. would receive the news, or if he would want to continue to keep it a secret. John Lloyd was determined to have a relationship with Will, regardless of how his father felt about, but he hoped that Will would be welcomed by the entire family. I thought that perhaps H.B. would be willing, maybe even happy, about the revelation that he had another son, but I knew that Annabelle would throw a major hissy-fit. This would not bode well for her self-perception as being Charleston's high society, beau monde queen.

We'd arranged to meet H.B. at the family's beach house on Sullivan's Island around noon. John Lloyd told his father that he had some important news for 'his ears only', which was their code for 'keep Annabelle in the dark'. This wasn't an entirely unusual scenario, so H.B. agreed to the meeting, no questions asked.

John Lloyd and I were supposed to travel over to the Isle of Palms together in the morning to meet with Jayne and her husband, who were vacationing there. We'd planned on meeting up with H.B. on Sullivan's Island after our brunch with the love birds.

I'd dreamt of Papa Joe the night before, he was rocking in that Father's Day chair, and he kept looking at me sadly, and shaking his head 'no'. I woke up sweating, and feeling disconcerted, like something was seriously amiss. I tried to shake it off as I readied myself for the day, but the picture of my grandfather kept coming into my mind. What had Papa Joe been trying to tell me, not to tell H.B.? Leave it to him to want to keep secrets, even from beyond the grave.

Early that morning, John Lloyd called to tell me that he'd been hung up with an important client, which I took to mean that he was shacked-up someplace with a lover, as he was known to do from time to time. He said he'd meet me at his family's beach house at noon, and asked me to give Jayne and Dylan his deepest apologies. He promised me that we'd get together with them before they headed back to Boston at the end of the week. Although Jayne and I had kept in touch, and she'd adored John Lloyd the few times she'd been in his company, I'd never shared the truth of our relationship with her. I realized that I'd never been totally honest with anyone about anything in my life, except for John Lloyd - the keeper of my conscience.

Jayne and Dylan were sorry to miss John Lloyd, but that didn't damper their enthusiasm for seeing me. Jayne danced me around the restaurant deck, as she squealed about how wonderful I looked and how much she had missed me. Jayne and her husband together seemed like the perfect couple, tanned, beautiful, and rich. Jayne's hair was highlighted, and her blue eyes were sparking. Dylan's reddish hair had natural highlights in its curls, and his eyes were the color of the ocean. I felt guilty about the pang of jealousy I'd experienced at seeing their beauty and happiness. It wasn't like me to be jealous of anyone, but there it was. I suppose it had to do with the fact that they believed John Lloyd to be my lover, and that he hadn't even bothered to show up. It didn't make any sense, I knew, but I felt embarrassed and hurt that he wasn't there with me, and I could feel myself becoming angry over his absence. Maybe that's what Papa Joe had been trying to tell me in my dream last night - that John Lloyd wasn't going to show up at all.

Jayne and Dylan had reserved a table for four on the terrace overlooking the dunes, where the three of us were served a brunch fit for kings. Jayne was sipping a mimosa and chatting amiably, but it was hard for me to concentrate on her stories. My mind was on John Lloyd, and it seemed to me that the sounds of the waves crashing upon the shore were speaking an ill omen. I kept looking at the empty fourth chair, imagining John Lloyd sitting there, and wishing that he had made the extra effort to be there with us. For some reason, probably the dream, I felt as though there was a black cloud hanging just over my head. I was sorry to have to cut the visit with Jayne and Dylan short, but I had to leave to meet with John Lloyd and H.B., so I promised them that we'd all get together in a few days. There are some promises in life that you can't help but break.

It was already quarter past noon when I got to the Maybank beach house, and John Lloyd's car wasn't there yet. The front door had been left unlocked, so I let myself in and found H.B. waiting, drink in hand, out on the screen porch. He was gazing out upon the breaking surf on this day that had become gray, hazy, and overcast. He was surprised to see that I had arrived alone, and motioned for me to help myself to a cocktail. When I told him that John

Lloyd was running late because of an important meeting with a client, H.B. gave me one of those 'down the nose' stares, which spoke of disbelief.

H.B. was an attractive older man. His blonde hair had grayed to a light, sandy color, and his steely eyes were that same robin's-egg blue as both John Lloyd's and Will's. We made small talk for about thirty minutes, during which time he'd repeatedly glanced at his watch. H.B. was getting impatient, and I couldn't blame him; my own anxiety was taking its toll on my stomach, which was churning. I excused myself to go and place a call to the gallery to find out the cause of John Lloyd's delay.

Janette, his receptionist, said that John Lloyd hadn't been in all morning, nor had he called. This wasn't totally unusual for John Lloyd, who had always come and gone as he pleased. What *was* unusual, was for him not to show up, or call us here at the beach house. I felt panic begin to rise up within me as I returned to H.B. on the porch. The wind blew his cigar smoke toward my face, and the cloud enveloped my head – a second black cloud, I thought, but I tried to sound casual, and keep from revealing my true emotion.

"I don't know what's keeping him, H.B.; it's not like him not to call when he's going to be late." I could hear the fear in my own voice, and realized that I wasn't fooling anyone.

H.B. looked at me coldly and asked, "Do you even know where he *really* is, Marra?"

"He only said that he was meeting with a client. He promised that he'd meet us here at noon," I said, with as much sincerity as I could muster.

"I think we've both waited long enough, and if this *news* that John Lloyd wants to share is so important, he'd have made an effort to get here on time. I have business to attend to. Y'all have him call me, and we'll arrange to meet later in the day." As he started toward the door, the phone rang.

"That'll be him calling to say that he's on his way, I'm sure!" I said eagerly.

But I was wrong. It wasn't John Lloyd, although it was about John Lloyd. His little convertible sports car had been sideswiped, and had careened off of the Silas Pearman Bridge an hour earlier when he'd been on his way here. The authorities hadn't wanted to notify Mr. Maybank until they had positively identified the body of, what they believed, was his only son.

In my mind's eye, I could see Papa Joe shaking his head. If I'd understood that he'd meant 'don't go', would I have postponed it? Would John Lloyd still be alive? Can we change our destiny?

CHAPTER SIXTEEN

The Maybank family preferred to wait ten, long, agonizing days before having a memorial service celebrating John Lloyd's twenty-nine years of life. The service was held at Trinity United Methodist Church, where the Maybanks had worshipped for generations. They'd asked me to be a part of the service, and to either speak, or sing. As intimidating as it is to get up and sing in front of an entire congregation, whom I knew would *all* be in attendance, it was preferable to speaking.

Dylan had to return to Boston, but Jayne graciously offered to stay with me for as long as I needed her. As difficult as it was for me to function with people around, it was impossible for me to be alone. The Serenity Prayer repeated itself in my head a thousand times, until I finally settled on my simple chant, '*Let it be*', and then I'd hear John Lloyd singing the Beatle's song, as clearly as though he were standing right next to me.

Edith stayed with Jayne and me at what used to be Papa Joe's, and was now my house. It was nice to have her there. She took charge and mothered me, and that was exactly what I needed. She would point me in a direction and tell me what to do; otherwise I would have been wandering around the house aimlessly. Edith and Jayne encouraged me to eat, bathe, dress, or lie down and rest at the appropriate times, as I moved about as if in a trance. I could hardly form a sentence or complete a thought; I felt as though my brain had short-circuited.

I hadn't heard from Brady in months, and I wasn't able to find her. It was like she'd fallen off of the face of the earth. She'd left her apartment and had left no forwarding address. According to Dino, she had abruptly quit her job at the restaurant and given them no reason. Her last pay check was still sitting there, waiting for her to claim it. I couldn't imagine where she had gone.

I wasn't surprised that Will came down for the service, especially now that he knew that John Lloyd had been his only brother, but I was shocked that Shelby had come along with him. They stayed at the Francis Marion Hotel on King Street, just blocks from the church. Edith had offered for her and Jayne to vacate, so that my family could stay here with me, but in truth, Jayne and Edith felt more like family to me than my siblings did.

The day after they'd arrived, Will and Shelby came over to visit with us. Edith had insisted upon preparing a formal luncheon for all of us. It was strange to me how much my siblings had aged since I'd seen them last, they weren't children anymore. I'm sure that they had thought the same of me. I asked Will if he was ready to share the secret with H.B. yet, but the timing didn't seem appropriate to him. Will was devastated that he'd never had the chance to meet his only brother. I witnessed the sorrow that was etched upon his face whenever we spoke of John Lloyd. Will was being kind and conciliatory towards me, and it seemed as though he was sincerely distraught over our loss.

Will had left home when I was just a kid, and I hadn't seen him, or heard from him, more than a dozen times over the years. It seemed strange to me that this thirty-four-year-old brother of mine was acting like we'd always been close, when in fact, we barely knew each other. I suppose that this nurturing attitude he'd suddenly developed toward me had more to do with John Lloyd's death than it did with me. Will was grieving for himself too. He had finally found a part of himself that had been missing, only to lose it before he could get a grip on it, so he was holding on to me instead. Although it felt a little strange to me, I really appreciated my brother's attention and sympathetic concern.

Shelby was her usual self, preoccupied with aesthetics and all that is superficial. I was disappointed that she hadn't brought the girls along, but under the circumstances, it wasn't an appropriate occasion for young children. I knew that John Lloyd's family would be taken with Shelby; she was a beautiful, hazel-eyed blonde, perfected coiffed and manicured, and looked fabulous in her designer apparel. She'd appreciate their wealth and fashion sense, whereas I couldn't care less about such things. If it hadn't been for John Lloyd, I would have shown up at his parent's house wearing jeans. He always chose my outfits, because I never had a clue about what to wear. He'd call me his *living Barbie doll'*, as he'd be choosing items from a store rack, or sorting through my closet. I'd learned so much from him, how to dress, which fork to use, and that there *are* people in the world you can trust.

Shelby hugged me stiffly, and said how sorry she was about John – and no matter how many times she'd hear him referred to as *John Lloyd*, she'd still call him John. I wondered whether she did things like that to irritate me, or if she was just clueless. To add insult to injury, she'd added, "It seems like death just follows you everywhere, Marra!"

Had Edith heard her, I'm sure she would have had a stinging remark to sling back in Shelby's direction, but there was no one around us. I never knew what to say to her in times like that, and I'd be hurting too much to think of a response.

I suppose I'd held out hope that Shelby would be warmer and more understanding towards me because of my grief, but no such luck. Shelby's thought process was impervious, as always. Once again, I was left wondering why she said such awful things to me.

I realized much later that I'd been in shock during that time; I really couldn't believe that he was gone. John Lloyd had been a constant in my life for over five years, and he had been closer to me than anyone had ever been. He wasn't a lover, but we had shared a love that even lovers seldom knew. He had known me better than I'd known myself - he was my compass, my barometer, my heart. I was lost without him, hopelessly, helplessly, lost. He had once read me an e.e. cummings poem that included the line, *"I carry your heart in my heart"*, and only *now* did I understand what that poem really meant – because now I carried *his* heart in my heart.

Will spent every day that he was in town with me. Shelby stayed busy exploring Charleston, seeking out the bargains she couldn't go home without. Will sat close to me as he read Mama's diary, asked me questions about the people in it, and studied his birth certificate. We walked the streets of Charleston together, and I showed him the place his parents were born and raised. He seemed genuinely interested in John Lloyd's life, and barraged me with questions about his lost brother, as he sat examining every photo I owned of him. I'd seen tears in Will's eyes just before he rose and hurried out the door. He'd lost something with John Lloyd's death, and as painful as that was for him, it would have been worse had he known him in life. John Lloyd's presence had been huge, taking up whatever space he occupied, so his absence created a vacuum, a huge void that sucked your heart away to a dark and empty place. I had loved other people in my lifetime, but no one had ever loved me the way that John Lloyd had, and I couldn't imagine anyone *ever* loving me that way again.

Edith seemed genuinely fond of Will, and fawned over him at every opportunity. She was incredulous that he'd never married, because he was *"such a handsome young man!"* At least three times a day I'd hear her tell him what a great catch he'd be for some lucky young lady. Will would blush with embarrassment at the compliments, as he smiled and cast his eyes downward. I realized then that Will was shy, something I'd never known about him.

I'd always assumed that Will was cold and aloof, because I'd never heard much from him, but he was proving that assumption wrong. He'd had a few long-term girlfriends over the years, but being career military, Will traveled frequently, and most relationships can't weather that much distance. It was good to spend the time with him and to be able to share John Lloyd's life stories with someone who was so genuinely interested.

The memorial service was difficult for everyone, as I'd known it would be. As he spoke, the minister kept mentioning me as John Lloyd's fiancé, information that had been transmitted by Annabelle, no doubt. Many of those in attendance stood, sharing stories and anecdotes regarding John Lloyd. They spoke of his astonishing compassion, and of his depth of kindness. They told stories illustrating his outrageous sense of humor, soothing us with the only comic relief of the day. They were all in agreement that the loss of this beautiful young man was just devastating.

I sat in a front pew between Jayne and Will, even though Annabelle had encouraged me to sit next to her. I knew that Annabelle had never really approved of me, but I'd always remained gracious in her presence for John Lloyd's sake, because she was his mother. I didn't have to play up to John Lloyd's family anymore, and for that one thing I was grateful. After the eulogy, which had been very eloquently delivered by H.B., the minister motioned me up onto the altar to perform my ode to John Lloyd. I sang the song that he'd sung to me at Missy's wedding, the same one that we'd sung to each other at Jayne's wedding, *Lovin' You.*

It was brutal to sing the words that no longer held true. There'd be no old age for him, no more sun reflected in the light of his eyes. I recalled that spring day I'd met him, his wolf-whistle, the deep dimples when he smiled, his blue, blue eyes, and the way he'd called *me* beautiful,

126

when in reality, it was *he* who was truly beautiful. I had once asked him why he'd pursued me that day, and he'd said, *"You looked so lost and sad, walkin' down that street all alone, I knew you needed me to love you, Marra Dallas."*

I managed to sing the song and stay on key, while the salty tears flowed onto my lips. I kept my eyes upon the antique dental molding of the ornate balcony over the entryway, when suddenly, John Lloyd appeared up there, smiling down at me. I smiled back at him, I was so happy that he'd chosen that moment to appear to me, looking so pleased that I was singing *our* song for him.

As I stepped down from the altar, I could hear men blowing their noses, and saw women dabbing at tears. H.B. came toward me, arms opened wide to enfold me in an embrace, which had taken me by surprise, because it was totally out of character for him.

"Thank you, darlin' girl, that was just amazin', he would have loved it," H.B. said, and then, looking earnestly into my eyes, he stated, "Y'all really did love him."

"Yes, I really did love him," I said, and the lump in my throat, burning like a slice from a hot knife, prevented me from saying anything more.

People milled around outside on the grand portico, leaning against the imposing Corinthian columns while waiting for a chance to extend condolences to the family and to me. It took some time to make our way through the sea of mourners and back to our vehicles. There'd been many voices in my ears, but I couldn't decipher what they'd said – I'd just nodded my head and kept walking.

The Maybank's reception at their fifteen-thousand square foot, three story, Federal-style mansion in Harleston Village was open to family and friends, which meant that half of Charleston was in attendance. Annabelle saw to it that every detail was faultless, the only thing she could do in order to avoid the emotional collapse that was inevitably approaching, like a storm sweeping in from the sea. John Lloyd's sister, Missy, had been in audible tears throughout the service, and continued in that same vein, causing me, among others, to avoid her like the plague.

More than once, John Lloyd had said that Missy majored in PDA – public displays of audacity. I believe it was because Missy was jealous of her brother. John Lloyd was charismatic, and his beauty and kindheartedness were captivating. Missy Maybank, on the other hand, though attractive in a severe and angular way, was callous and shrill. If she wasn't the center of attention, she'd cause a scene to upstage whoever was. Like her mother, Missy was cool to me, but wouldn't dare chance alienating her brother by being obviously offensive. I think that both Annabelle and Missy had coveted my intimacy with John Lloyd, the son and brother they'd never really understood.

H.B. had been working his way around the room greeting family and friends when he'd noticed our arrival. I'd seen him stealing glances at Will in the church, and now he kept looking from the man who was holding onto his shoulder, over to Will, and back again. I could see that there was recognition, or familiarity, when H.B. looked at Will's face. I could see H.B. excusing himself to come over to us; he wanted to know who Will was, if he didn't already.

H.B. stood beside me as I made the introductions - my friend Jayne, her mother Edith, my sister Shelby, and my brother Will. I saw that H.B. had barely made eye contact with the women, but held Will's gaze as he shook his hand and searched his face, recognizing the features he saw there. H.B. knew, I could see it in his eyes, that Will was his son. It all came together for him now.

I knew that I favored Mama, especially when H.B. had guessed at first glance that I was Charlotte Whitford's daughter. The first time that John Lloyd had taken me home to meet his family, H.B. had looked at me as though he'd seen a ghost. He'd even *accidentally* called me Charlotte a few times over the years, admitting that he'd known my mother, but not elaborating on their relationship. I saw the sorrow in his expression when I'd told him that Mama had been murdered, and the tears in his eyes as he'd turned away and excused himself. H.B.'s reaction to me, and to Mama's fate, caused me to believe that he'd loved her. Annabelle had feigned surprise when

H.B. informed her that I was Charlotte's daughter, but I knew that she had already figured that out. Just as H.B. had greeted me wistfully, Annabelle had accepted me grudgingly. I was the daughter of her adversary, and even though she'd won the prize, in the form of H.B. Maybank as her husband, I'm not sure that she'd ever won his heart. Just like H.B. had been the love of Mama's life, it was quite possible that she had been the love of his.

After studying my brother Will's face intently, H.B. leaned over and whispered in my ear, *"This was what y'all were fixin' to tell me, about Will."* When his eyes met mine again, I nodded and smiled, and he took my hand in his, squeezed it, and smiled back. I felt as though I'd given him a gift, a son found for a son lost. I wondered if he'd known, or suspected, that Mama had been pregnant back then. After all, she'd suddenly been whisked away to the St. Agnes Home for Girls. Back in those days, when girls 'disappeared' to visit relatives for a matter of months or more, people knew what that meant. Maybe someday H.B. would confide in me, and I'd have a bigger picture of Mama's life, I thought.

I stood gazing out of the large, mullioned, tiffany windows that stood open toward the courtyard below. I saw my sister and Edith chatting, as they wandered around the estate, admiring flowers, fountains and statuary, with cigarettes in one hand and cocktails in the other. Jayne had stayed close by me, for which I was grateful. She warded off the constant barrage of mourners, who all seemed determined, for some reason, to touch me, as they shared their own personal John Lloyd stories. Jayne kept offering me a drink, saying it would make me feel better, but I knew that nothing had that power. I was waiting to wake up from this awful nightmare, to be told that none of it was real, and that John Lloyd was coming home at any moment . . . if only . . .

H.B. and Will had disappeared down a hallway together, and when they returned almost an hour later, I feigned a migraine in order to escape. I was anxious to hear about their conversation, but I wouldn't pry; I'd wait for Will to share whatever he would, when he was ready. Shelby was the first to leave for home, and a few days later Edith and Jayne left too, at my insistence. Although they'd offered to stay with me for as long as I needed them, I knew that Jayne had a husband and a job to get home to, and that Edith had her own life waiting for her. Once they'd left, Will stayed on with me for another week and helped me to figure out what to do next. It was time for me to move on; Charleston held too much sadness for me now.

Papa Joe's house was sold and my belongings were in a moving van headed toward Florida. As I drove south, I thought about the knock on the door the day before by my handsome, surprise visitor, Jason, John Lloyd's lover. We embraced, brought together by the shared grief of losing the one we had both loved. It was an intimate moment with a total stranger, and those moments don't happen often in life, if ever.

Jason told me that he felt as though he knew me because of all that John Lloyd had told him about me. Jason spoke of pictures he'd seen of John Lloyd and me together, and described some of the momentous occasions I'd shared with John Lloyd, as if he had been present himself. If he was waiting for me to return the sentiment, he had to have been disappointed. What could I have possibly said to him? John Lloyd had never so much as mentioned his name to me, not that I could recall. Or had he, and had I chosen not to pay attention to him? Had I blocked it out because I didn't want to know about any life that John Lloyd had that didn't include me? Suddenly I realized how self-centered I'd been in my relationship with John Lloyd, it had always been about me. John Lloyd had made me feel special, without ever expecting anything at all in return. He'd loved me unconditionally, and allowed me to draw my parameters around our relationship. I didn't want to know about his love life with Jason, and so he didn't speak about it to me. He'd been a much better friend to *me* than I'd ever been to *him*. I said a silent apology to my friend, my angel, and heard his voice in my mind say, *"It's okay, baby girl."*

Jason had begged me to stay in touch with him, and I'd promised that I would, but I couldn't really imagine that happening. He was trying to keep John Lloyd alive by holding on to me, but for me it would have been much too painful. I had become very adept at moving on and not looking back, lest I become a pillar of salt.

H.B. and Will had spent some time together before Will returned to his new assignment in Tampa. I didn't know if H.B. had shared the knowledge of his new son with the rest of his family at that point. Will didn't seem to care about getting to know Missy, or any of the other Maybank family members, but maybe he would in time. I hoped that H.B. wasn't trying to replace John Lloyd with Will, but I didn't share my concern with my brother, he had enough on his plate right now.

I was still a little unsure of how it all was going to work, my living with Will; but he had assured me that I'd have the place to myself most of the time because of all the traveling he did. I wasn't sure what I'd do for work, although Will was certain that I'd have no problem getting a teaching position with the local community college since I'd recently received my Master of Education degree.

Heading south on I-95 in my black Cressida with my *Who's Next* tape blaring, I knew that it was the appropriate time for me to be moving on. All that had been my life in Charleston was gone. That song was over, it was all behind me, I should have known that death would find me - and Roger Daltrey sang to the wide open spaces and the infinite sea.

PART IV

1987, Age 33

Flying Lessons

Looking back, my life seemed like a series of endings and new beginnings. If I had to describe it thus far, it would be transitory: not permanent or lasting, but existing in fits and starts. Sometimes, even in the most transitory lifestyle, there are changes that take place that break our patterns.

Death had seemed to be the one constant in my life thus far, and my traveling companions had been the specters of those I'd loved and lost. I've learned that the deaths of some of our relationships are sometimes as painful as a physical death.

But with age and experience comes a wisdom that is honed and sharpened by the sword of pain that pierces our hearts, and tempered by the tears that flow from our rivers of sadness. I've also learned that although some of us are destined for a life filled with acute pain and much disappointment, there are also blessings, and that those blessings can more than compensate for all of the burdens that we are obliged to bear.

CHAPTER SEVENTEEN

Six years earlier . . .

The condo I shared with Will on Dunedin causeway was owned by an Air Force colonel and his wife, who were now stationed in Hawaii. They let Will rent it month-to-month for next to nothing because they knew that Will would take good care of it, and because this wasn't a property that you'd want to sell off. Beach properties were at a premium, especially in this location.

The causeway was a two-and-a-half mile narrow strip of land that began at the mainland and extended out into the Gulf of Mexico via the St. Joseph Sound, up to the entrance of Honeymoon Island State Park. The state park was filled with natural, sun-drenched beaches, mangrove swamps, and tidal flats. There was a section of the causeway called Dog Beach, where pups could roam free, and enjoy the warm gulf waters. There was a ferry to Caladesi Island, an unspoiled piece of land surrounded by sparking gulf waters. It was best for shelling because it was only accessible by boat.

Will was seldom home, so I had the place to myself ninety percent of the time. The first few months seemed like an extended vacation, one that I felt I was entitled to after all I'd been through. I'd lay by the pool, or on the beach, or walk on the nature trails. I took to collecting shells, starfish, and interesting stones, and then drying them out on the deck railing. The smell of salt had permeated everything I owned, and I had to learn to live with the grit of sand underfoot, even in the carpeting.

The third month I was there I met Corey Reynolds, a part-time student, bartender, and aspiring artist. He spent more time on the beach than anyplace else, leaving him with a deep tan, and long, sun-streaked, curly hair. He was originally from Townsend, Tennessee, a small town on the west side of the Smoky Mountains. He was so mellow that he made laid-back seem hyperactive. He never wore a watch or made plans for tomorrow. His favorite phrase was, *"Chill, man."*

At twenty-five, Corey was two years younger than me, but told me that age was just a number, and he was just what the doctor ordered. Ours was a purely fun, physical relationship with no goals. I had no desire to plan for a future, and Corey didn't believe in the future anyway, only in the now. He was in my life for nine, fun-filled months. Most of our time together was spent on the beach, at the beach bar, or in bed. Corey asked no questions, gave no explanations, and expected nothing, other than enjoying life to the fullest. For brief periods of time I was able to disconnect from my feelings, and merely enjoy life with him. It was healing for me to just *be*, and not think.

Will never met Corey, but questioned why I hadn't pursued finding a job in all that time.

"I have plenty of money to live on, and I'm not ready to move on with my life just yet," I told my brother, "I need time to get over losing John Lloyd!" I'd said, as if that were even a possibility.

"I'm sorry, Marra, I just want you to be happy. I feel like you're wallowing in your grief. I understand that you're still hurting, but you need to start healing. I know that I abandoned you when you were a kid, and I'm sorry about that. I'm trying to make that up to you now," he said.

"Will, you have nothing to apologize for. You were only a kid yourself, and you needed to find your own way. I appreciate everything that you're doing for me, truly. I'll find a job soon, and I'll move on with my life soon, you'll see!" I promised.

Will returned to Charleston a few times, and had spent some weekends with H.B. on Sullivan's Island. They were getting to know each other as father and son, as well as friends. I didn't ask many questions, but Will shared that he was happy to have that connection in his life. He said that he'd never felt like Bill Dunne was a father to him. He thought that Bill (formerly known as Daddy) preferred his daughters to his son, and that had always bothered Will. It had hurt Will's self-esteem, because every young boy needs his daddy's approval. I told Will that I'd never felt that Daddy had cared much for me either, but I suppose that was little consolation to a boy who'd grown up with a distant father. Will seemed to want to talk about the past, but I'd always change the subject, and then find some excuse to rush out.

I was, as usual, trying to move on with my life and leave the past behind, just as I'd always done. Will's connection to the Maybanks wasn't easy for me to deal with either, but I didn't want to rain on his parade. He'd been good to me, taking me in, and allowing me to start over in a new place. I needed time to adjust to a new beginning, to be able to put the past behind me once again and start over with a clean slate.

I found that it was comforting to sit by the warm gulf waters and watch the sun set, as it turned the sky into a kaleidoscope of colors that were caught in the white, puffy clouds to the east. The salty aroma in the gentle breeze and the feel of the warm sand between my toes helped to sooth my tortured soul.

Gazing out toward the horizon, I'd glimpse John Lloyd standing in the surf, pointing to the dolphin fins that would arc up out of the water, not thirty feet away from me. He'd smile at me and twirl around, indicating the beauty that surrounded me as if to say, *"Be happy, Marra Dallas, you've got all this."* I'm trying, John Lloyd, I'm trying.

CHAPTER EIGHTEEN

In 1982, Shelby came to Florida for a week with her kids when Darcy was eleven, and Deidre was three and a half. Naturally, the kids wanted to go to Disney World, Sea World, Busch Gardens and, of course, to the beach. Will had taken the week off, and for seven days I actually felt like I was a part of a real family, doing all of the things that families do. Will was great with the kids, and I kept thinking that he really should find someone and settle down, he was thirty-six already!

The kids were adorable, and Shelby was a devoted mother, although she'd been a bit obsessive about the girls being well-groomed at all times. She reminded me of Mama, and I could picture her with a steamy curling iron

141

in one hand, and pink lip gloss in the other, chasing them around the house to beautify them to her specifications.

Darcy still favored me, and walking hand in hand with her in Disney World, I'm sure that people thought she was mine. Little Deidre was platinum blonde, with big, brown eyes, the picture of Shelby at that age. It was obvious that Shelby favored Deidre, and treated Darcy as though she were only there to help take care of her little sister. I don't think Shelby realized how transparent she was. She'd constantly criticize Darcy, while fawning over Deidre, but if Darcy's feelings were hurt, she never let on. Mother's little helper would make herself indispensible, and keep her mama happy at all times. *'Good luck with that'*, I thought!

At first, I tried to compensate by building Darcy up, or doing something special just for her. Invariably, Shelby would chastise me, and say that it wasn't fair that I'd gotten something for Darcy and left poor Deidre out, even if it was something that would not have been age-appropriate for the little one. I knew that I could not explain my motives to Shelby, because to do so would have been to criticize her, and I would never have done that in a million years; after all, how would I ever win favor with my only sister if I made her mad at me?

No matter how hard I tried, things were just as chilly as they'd always been between my sister and me. Our conversations remained superficial and, as always,

Shelby seemed to be critical of just about everything that came out of my mouth, so I kept my opinions to a minimum in order to keep the peace. It wasn't easy, if I said black, she'd say white. There were times when I wanted to corner her and ask her what the hell her problem was with me, but instead I'd just repeat the Serenity Prayer inside my head, and then I'd hear John Lloyd singing *Let It Be*.

I almost lost it one day after she'd jumped down my throat because I'd commented on how dark Deidre's eyes were. I thought that because Albert had blue eyes and Shelby had hazel eyes, both of the girls would have lighter eyes. Shelby pointed out that hazel was in the brown family, and that she didn't understand why I always had to be such a know-it-all. I really would have liked to slap her upside the head, but as usual, I let it go. The girls didn't want to leave at the end of the week, and made Shelby promise that she'd bring them back again soon. As much as I'd enjoyed the company of the little ones, I was relieved for my sister to be going. Her presence seemed to always cause me great anxiety.

After Corey left town I decided it was time for me to grow up and get a job. I was twenty-eight, and it was *'high time'*, as Mama used to say. I got a position at the local community college as an adjunct instructor, teaching Humanities. It had not been my first choice, but it was all that was available at the time. I had three classes a week, so I still had plenty of free time to enjoy the beach.

I'd gotten in the habit of having breakfast at Kelly's on Main Street almost every morning. It was a funky little place that had great food and an eclectic array of patrons. I could read the newspaper or a book, and nobody would bother me. Or, I could have a conversation with a server, who'd pull up a chair on his break and give a dissertation on the declining moral fabric of American society: We were a less friendly, more judgmental nation than we'd ever been. Whatever gains had been made in the '60s were lost in the '80s, where it seemed that the motto was *'Every Man for Himself'*. The most interesting thing was that these conversations were taking place inside of an establishment that seemed to be more of the '60s genre, more of a 'Live and Let Live' society. I much preferred it to the rest of the world.

I'd become friendly with a pilot named Dean who, like me, ate breakfast at Kelly's almost every morning. He'd struck up a conversation with me one day when he noticed that I'd been reading Robert Ludlum's *The Parsifal Mosaic*, and asked for my critique. He'd become an avid reader on his frequent layovers, when there was little to do but wait on whomever he was taxiing around the world. Our discussions began about books, but eventually I learned that he was a Florida native who like to spin tall tales about the 'old days' – before all of us damn Yankees had invaded. Although he was a young man, something about Dean reminded me of Papa Joe, and I found that quite endearing.

When I mentioned to him that I'd always wanted to learn to fly, Dean generously offered to give me free flying lessons at the small local airfield. I was starting to get excited about the prospect of piloting a small plane by myself, but before I could receive my first lesson Dean became otherwise engaged. It seemed that Dean's career had included flying illegal substances into the country, and he'd been captured and was going to be detained for the next few years - so much for earning my wings!

Over the course of our association, Dean had introduced me to many of his acquaintances, one of whom was his friend Heather, who dined with him weekly. Heather was also a Florida native, who fancied herself an artist. From what I perceived of her art, it seemed more like arts and crafts – she'd glue bits of detritus she'd found on the beach onto a canvas and then add a few splashes of watercolors.

Heather was the type who invaded your personal space, that two-foot, invisible circumference we all have surrounding our physical body that is usually reserved for those with whom we are intimate. Heather declared herself my 'kindred spirit', and implied that we had, perhaps, been great friends in another lifetime. I remember thinking, *'Yeah, must have been another lifetime, cause I just ain't feelin' it in this one!'*

Heather plied me with personal questions, which even in the best of circumstances made me uncomfortable.

I was perturbed, but not surprised, when she showed up at the condo one morning with a bunch of wildflowers and a bag of whole wheat bagels. She was trying hard to be my friend, which I couldn't quite understand. Here she was in her own home town, where she should have already had a slew of friends. I suppose that was a sign of sorts that should have sent up red flags; but I believed her to be harmless, and so did nothing to discourage her friendship.

Will had met her a few times, and I could see by the looks exchanged between them that there was a mutual attraction. She really was a very pretty girl, so it didn't surprise me that Will had found her attractive. I didn't believe anything would ever come of it though, as they were so entirely different. Goes to show you what I know.

There were a few young teachers I'd become friendly with as well, and we'd occasionally go out for drinks to an upscale pub. Most of those places were meat markets - you couldn't sit at the bar for five minutes and have a conversation without getting hit on. A lot of the single women, and even a few married ones, were more than thrilled by the attention that we'd garner from the solicitous gentlemen, who were either looking for Ms. Right, or a quick roll in the hay. I certainly wasn't looking for a roll, or a relationship, and was content to be out on the beach with a good book, but fate had other plans.

CHAPTER NINETEEN

I met Captain Jack McNeil, USMC, when he came to lecture at our campus. He'd written a book that I'd read and found extremely interesting, *Far and Away*, about the rescue of the US Embassy hostages in Tehran. He had my undivided attention throughout his speech.

He was fortyish, with salt and pepper hair, steely gray-blue eyes, narrow face, and a slim build. He was handsome in a boyish way, but he had a commanding presence. He'd made eye contact with me several times during his presentation, and I remember thinking what a great lecturer he was. Eye contact was something I'd have to remind myself about whenever I lectured my class.

After the lecture, his fans gathered around him to ask questions and to get autographs. As much as I would have liked to have joined them, I wasn't comfortable in a crowd, so I ducked out and went down to Severs' Hall, where the reception for Captain McNeil would take place shortly. I owned his book, and had considered bringing it along for an autograph, but I knew that I'd never have the nerve to ask, so I'd left it at home on the coffee table. I kept myself busy reading the program our Word Processing department had created for the occasion. It contained a brief bio of John Patrick 'Jack' McNeil: *Born and raised in Burbank, California, quarterback UCLA, United States Naval Academy, TBS at Quantico, served in Cambodia, Vietnam, Lebanon, Iran, El Salvador, Libya, and most recently in Egypt.* I found it interesting that he was currently stationed at MacDill Air Force Base, where my brother Will was also stationed.

Captain McNeil came in with his entourage in tow, and met my eye with a wink and a half-smile. A few of the women I taught with joined me at my table, as did Vince, the director of our Physical Education department; he loved being the only male in the midst of a gaggle of women. He'd say he loved the scent of the 'essence of estrogen', but really, he was just a horny dog looking to get laid. Connie Harmon, the creative writing instructor, had succumbed to his wiles and lived to regret it. A college campus is a microcosm of gossip, rumor, and innuendo. It happened on a Friday night, and by Monday morning the tawdry news of their affair was all over our campus. Embarrassed by her lapse of good judgment, Connie transferred to the St. Petersburg Campus the next semester, leaving Vince behind to brag about his latest conquest.

A few times, it appeared as though Captain McNeil was making his way over toward my table, but each time he'd get close someone would intervene and corner him in conversation. It was getting late, and I was tired of the small talk and gossip and was ready to head outside for some fresh air. I said goodbye to the women around me and did my best to slink out the door without being intercepted. I hurried down the empty corridor, stilettos echoing as they hammered the polished terrazzo, and then I heard a man's voice calling, "Wait up!"

I turned and saw Captain McNeil jogging toward me.

"Where are you going? We haven't even met yet," he said with a grin.

"Sorry," I said with a smile, "it was getting late, and you always seemed to be surrounded by the masses." I held my hand out to him, "Marra Dallas, Humanities."

He smiled, and his blue eyes crinkled at the corners.

"Your last name is Humanities?" he chuckled.

"No, I teach Humanities. Sorry, I'm so used to introducing myself that way here. I suppose it's like name, rank, and serial number, right? Anyway, I really enjoyed your lecture, Captain McNeil."

"It's Jack," he said. Still holding onto my hand, he moved closer to me, leaned in, and asked conspiratorially, "Would you like to go somewhere and grab a bite to eat? I'm starving."

Well, this was interesting! I was flattered, out of everyone who had fawned all over him tonight, he'd chosen me to ask to dinner. We went to a steak house near campus that was dark and quiet. They'd sat us in a corner booth with a candle burning on the table, and we drank red wine and ate rare steaks, and crisp, green salads. I told him about Will being stationed at MacDill, and Jack thought that was quite a coincidence; he said it must have been fate that had brought us together. Now he had my full attention, after all, fate and I were close companions.

Jack was fascinating to listen to, he had stories about situations he'd been in all over the world. He knew so many interesting people, and he spoke several languages. I could not imagine why he would want to spend time with someone like me, but he certainly seemed interested. We saw each other several times a week over the next six months, and Jack would keep me fascinated recounting his missions and exploits. He would always comment on what great a listener I was, and that may have been part of my charm for him. It didn't take me long to realize that Jack enjoyed being the center of attention. When Jack asked about my past, I'd skimmed over my childhood and was vague about my time in Charleston. I told him that I'd gone there after high school for college and lived with my grandfather, which was a sort-of truth. I led him to believe that I was a basic, boring academic, head buried in a book most of the time, and he seemed to take that at face value. Because I was so much younger, he must have assumed that I hadn't had much life experience to share anyway, and I encouraged him to believe just that. I knew that I was being less than honest with him, but in trying to reinvent myself, I'd decided to leave all of the unpleasant memories behind. I was operating on a 'need to know' basis, and I didn't believe that Jack needed to know any of the awful truths of my past.

Jack shared that he'd been married and divorced twice, and had a ten-year-old daughter, Katie, with his first wife. His little girl lived in Carlsbad, California, with her mother and step-father. He only admitted that his second marriage had been a 'misstep' on both of their parts, but neglected to share any of the details. I never pressed him for any information, because in doing so, I'd be opening myself up for cross-examination. Jack simply explained that his military career had always come first, and that he'd learned the hard way that women don't like to play second fiddle.

Jack, as Mama used to say, wined and dined me, and I became familiar with all of the best restaurants in the area. We'd frequent my favorite, The Beachcomber, on

Clearwater Beach, in addition to Armani's on the bay, Mise En Place in Tampa, and Bon Appétit in Dunedin. We celebrated my thirtieth birthday at Bern's Steak House, after Jack had taken me on the grand tour of the base. I was smitten with his attention, as he'd brush my hair behind my ear with his fingers and say, "You are such a pretty girl, Marra Dallas!"

Jack was handsome, generous, and a gentleman. He didn't put the moves on me for several weeks, although we'd had some serious, what Mama would have called, 'heavy pettin' sessions', which kept me from considering that he might be gay. Once you've lost one love to the other team, you're always on guard for that sort of thing. He was not the lover that James or Corey had been, but he was interesting and exciting. There was a sweetness about him when he wasn't boasting, something he had the tendency to do.

Will and Jack got along like brothers, so Jack and I went on double dates a few times with Will and his current squeeze, the artist Heather, for whom he'd fallen like a ton of bricks. The guys would inevitably talk 'military', and Heather and I would talk movies and books, although her literary knowledge was somewhat limited.

Heather was my age, tall, and a blued-eyed blonde who looked more like Will than I did. She called him William, and stared at him like he was the second coming. I was surprised that they'd hit it off so well. Heather was the hippie-type; peasant blouses, long, tie-dyed skirts, and toe-ring sandals. Will was your typical buttoned-down, straight arrow, clean-cut military guy. I suppose it's true that opposites do attract, but I'd never have put those two together. I'm sure she must have informed him that they were soul mates from another lifetime. Ugh!

Although I was less than delighted over Will's fascination with Heather, which he seemed to be oblivious about, Will seemed thrilled about my relationship with Jack. He probably had been worried that he'd be saddled with me forever. The fact that Jack was military was a major bonus for Will, he was not only getting rid of his little sister, he was gaining a buddy in the process.

Jack's house was in South Tampa, and I'd stay there with him whenever Will was at home. I'd extricate myself from the condo, not only to give Will and Heather their privacy, but because seeing them together made me uncomfortable, for whatever reason. I couldn't put my finger on it, but there was something about Heather that brought out a critical spirit in me, and I didn't like the way that made me feel. I could plainly see that Will was in love with her, and although I wasn't thrilled about it, I wanted my brother to be happy.

Aside from my discomfort around Will's choice of female companionship, I was actually starting to enjoy my life again. Then one day, both Will and Jack were called to duty in the Persian Gulf after the Saudis had shot down two Iranian fighter planes in a protected shipping zone. Jack kept telling me that war was brewing in that part of the world, and that sooner or later, the shit was going to hit the fan. One of them being called out would have been scary, but both of them going was downright nerve-wracking.

It was during the time Will and Jack were deployed that I discovered that I was pregnant. I didn't have the feeling of dread that I'd had the first time, but of joy, coupled with a great sense of relief. I think there was a part of me that believed I'd blown it; I'd had my chance to be a mother, and tossed it back in God's face. Perhaps I believed that I'd be punished for what I'd done. But here I was, thirty-years-old, and I was going to have this baby, regardless of how Jack felt about it.

It turned out that Jack was delighted, and proposed to me on the spot. I said yes because I loved him, not because I was pregnant. I knew it would never be the kind of love that I'd shared with John Lloyd, because that was a once-in-a-lifetime love, but Jack and I enjoyed an easy relationship. Intellectually, we seemed evenly matched. Our personalities, though very different, meshed well. Jack was the showman, and I enjoyed observing him. When he was 'on', he could hold the attention of an entire room full of people. I suppose I'd felt a sense of pride just in being with him. Here he was, a big war hero, with a multitude of interesting tales that would captivate his audience, with me - quiet, shy little me. We had a small private ceremony with a Justice of the Peace, and had Will and Heather as our witnesses. Will gave me a hard time about keeping my own name, but I figured that I'd paid good money for this name, and I didn't want to waste it. Papa Joe would have been delighted with my sense of fiscal responsibility.

After we had spent a week on Sanibel Island for our honeymoon, I moved into Jack's house in Tampa. It was a lovely condo, with pine floors, high ceilings, and lots of light. It was centrally located in South Tampa, within walking distance to shops and restaurants. My first order of business was to decorate the nursery, and since we'd decided that we wanted to be surprised, the nursery was yellow, accents to be added later.

CHAPTER TWENTY

John Dallas 'J.D.' McNeil was born on Valentine's Day 1985, weighing in at an even nine pounds. Jack was thrilled to have a son, and I felt, for the first time in my life, that my fate had changed for the better.

I never realized that I could love anyone as much as I loved this cute little guy. He had curly brown hair, light blue eyes, and cheeks that looked like they were storing up nuts for the winter. There were dimples in his cheeks when he smiled, and a cleft in his chin, and there were dimples in his chubby little hands where his knuckles should have been. He only cried when he was, as Jack would say, *'poohed-up'*, but that wasn't often, because I'd usually smell it before he'd had the chance to let us know.

Shelby came down with the girls and stayed at Will's house, but she would bring the girls over to play with J.D. almost every day. The girls adored him, and the feeling was mutual. He'd shriek with joy when he saw them, lifting his little arms up to them, and they'd carry him around like a doll. They'd call him *'Chubby Bubbly'* because of the drool that constantly ran down his jowls, and he'd giggle, and spew his baby-slime all over himself. We joined them at Busch Gardens, where the girls took turns pushing the baby stroller, but Disney was out of the question, J.D. was too little for that yet.

Shelby seemed to adore my baby, which surprised me, because I didn't remember her being that loving with her own babies. She was full of advice, all of which I appreciated, even though it all sounded so critical. It seemed as though Shelby and I finally had something in common, something to connect us the way sisters should be connected, but that we'd never shared. I'd always craved her acceptance, but she'd always kept herself distant from me, as if she disapproved of me somehow.

Her little girls were adorable, and sweet as ever, and they'd called me Marra Dallas, rather than Auntie, or some other endearment. I wasn't sure how that had come about, and I wondered if that was how Shelby referred to me when she spoke about me, telling them, *'we're going to visit Marra Dallas'* not *'Auntie Marra'*.

Regardless of my failure to connect with my sister, I felt a bond with her children, and I was sorry to see them leave. Shelby still favored her younger daughter, as always, and Darcy now seemed to be aware of it in a way that she had been oblivious to earlier in life. I would notice Darcy rolling her large, green eyes when Shelby would fawn over Deidre. Darcy was still very sweet to her little sister, so she wasn't taking out on her, but I wondered what it would do to their relationship later in life. That wondering caused me to reflect back on my childhood memories of Mama fawning over Shelby. Was it possible that I was always jealous of Shelby? I had looked up to my older sister and tried to emulate her, but I couldn't conjure up any feelings of animosity for my sister, only her animosity toward me. It seemed that I'd spent the better part of my childhood trying to please her to the point where she'd finally realize how nice I was, so that she'd like me - all to no avail.

Shelby's visit proved to be another failed attempt to connect with my sister and, as always, I'd swear that I wouldn't go through that again. I'd tell myself that I was done trying to win her favor and that if she couldn't accept me, then so be it, I didn't need her in my life. Even as the thought formed, there was a part of me that knew I'd never give it up.

CHAPTER TWENTY~ONE

Heather had moved in with Will, who had tried more than once to buy the condo on the causeway from the colonel and his wife. They had finally agreed to sell to him, and it was only after Will had closed on the property that Heather began to push him for a ring. I suppose that should have been a sign that she had more in mind than just Will's love, but as they say - love is blind, and so Will bought her the largest diamond he could afford.

I'd gone back to teaching my three classes a week, Monday, Wednesday, and Friday evenings from seven until ten. With my commute from Tampa it would get me home by eleven, as long as I didn't get stuck with a student who needed to speak with me. Jack was always good about watching the baby when he was home, but I'd known from the start that there would be times he'd be out of town or hung up at the base until after I had to leave the house, so I'd found a local sitter.

Moira Hawthorn-Thwaite was an older British lady who had been living in Tampa for a dozen years. She was a spry grandmother who adored children, and I was lucky to have found her. It was Jack who had encouraged me to go back to work, not for the money, he'd said, but so that I'd have a sense of accomplishment. I'd felt as though I didn't need anything in my life other than my precious baby, but I'd always believed that Jack was wiser than I was, and so I'd returned to teaching. Jack and I had settled into a comfortable life. When he was home, Jack was usually in good spirits and was especially great with the baby. We'd still go out to restaurants, but not like we did before he was born. There were a great many local places that had outdoor dining, and those were the ones we'd frequent when we brought the baby out with us. Our life together was fulfilling for me; Jack was intelligent and interesting, always telling stories about exotic places and people. I had my career, and most of all, a precious baby boy whom I loved more than life itself.

In hindsight, I suppose that I'd always known that I'd never have the real closeness with Jack that I'd had with John Lloyd - he'd been the only person to whom I'd bared my soul. But I thought perhaps that had more to do with John Lloyd's being gay. None of the married women that I worked with seemed to be enamored with their husbands, and they all thought that Jack was *so* wonderful and that I was *so* lucky to have him, so I took my relationship at face value. It was what it was, and what that seemed to be was good enough for me. It was a comfortable relationship, everybody was happy, or so I'd thought.

The week before J.D.'s second birthday, and two months before Will and Heather's wedding, Moira left for her annual vacation to London. Jack told me that he'd be working late all week, so I was stuck for a sitter. I'd considered taking that week off, but Heather insisted that she'd love to help me out, as she had several times before. Will was out of town anyway, and Heather had always been good with the baby, so I took her up on her generous offer. I remember thinking that although she was flaky as hell, she'd always been kind to me, and that I should give her more credit for being a nice person.

Driving over the causeway from Tampa to Clearwater in the rain, I was thinking that I should be happier about my life than I felt. I had a husband who loved me, a wonderful baby son, a career that I enjoyed, and I'd reconnected with my siblings; but there was always a nagging doubt, like the other shoe was about to drop. I'd taken enough psychology classes to know that most of my doubts and fears stemmed from the tumultuous childhood I'd survived, and from the fact that I'd never had a sense of security - so each time these thoughts would creep up, I'd tell myself that I was being ridiculous, and do my little chant. Inevitably, I'd hear John Lloyd's sultry voice singing, *"Let it be . . ."*

When I got to the Clearwater side of the bay, I saw that a storm had recently passed over the area. Everything on the west side of the bay was dark, wet, and gloomy. When I pulled into the college parking lot, I noticed that most of the lights were off and that there were very few cars about. It turned out that all classes had been cancelled due to heavy thunderstorms and a tornado watch, but a few of us hadn't gotten the message in time. I hung around for a few minutes talking to some of the other instructors and to a few of the students who'd turned up, and then got into my car and headed back over to Tampa.

I was feeling bad that Heather had come all the way over to my place to watch the baby, only to have to turn around and go back home. Maybe she'd stay and have a glass of wine with me and hang out for a little while, I thought, as I was sure that my little angel would be fast asleep by the time I got home.

When I pulled onto our street, I saw Jack's little sports car in its spot, and thought perhaps he'd gotten in earlier than he'd anticipated. At first, I assumed that he'd already sent Heather home, but then I noticed that her car was still where it had been parked when I'd left. I tiptoed inside so I wouldn't wake the baby, in case he wasn't fully asleep yet. There was only one light on in the living room and the baby's door was closed, as was my bedroom door. I checked the empty kitchen, and even peeked outside the back door, thinking that maybe they'd gone out there to talk so as not to disturb the baby. When I saw that Jack and Heather weren't outside, or inside, that I could see, the feeling of dread hit me, and my stomach, as well as the other shoe, dropped.

I had to take a deep breath to calm myself before I opened my bedroom door, knowing what I was about to find on the other side. My heart was pounding in my chest, and my head was spinning; I felt sick to my stomach. I didn't want to do it, but I had to, I had no choice. I turned the handle, and flipped on the light.

To his credit, my startled husband jumped off of Heather immediately, saying, "Oh, shit, Marra, I'm so sorry, I'm so sorry!"

Heather, on the other hand, lay in my bed, stark naked, smirking at me as though she was very pleased with herself. There was no shame in her eyes, but rather a look of triumph, as though she'd beat me at a game of chess. My eyes went from Jack, back to Heather, and back again. I had to convince myself that what I was witnessing was real, because it all felt so surreal. It wasn't until Jack touched my arm that I came back to reality, turned, and walked away, into the baby's room, locking the door behind me.

I slid down the wall, and sat on the floor in the darkened room, the little blue Grover nightlight was glowing faintly in the corner. I could hear Jack talking to Heather outside the door, perhaps in the hallway. I heard him saying, "God damn it, Heather, you *have* to go now!" as if he were commanding her to do something she didn't want to do. Maybe she thought we'd all sit together and sing *Kum Ba Yah*, or maybe, being my 'kindred spirit', she'd expected a threesome!

Questions flooded my mind, *"How long has this been going on? How could I have been so clueless? What would I say to Will? Would he marry her anyway? Where will I go from here?"*

I could hear Jack on the other side of the door, quietly pleading with me to come out and talk to him. He kept saying, "I'm sorry, Marra. I didn't mean to, it just happened. I'm so sorry Marra. Please, come out here and talk to me. Marra, I'm sorry. I love you."

Yeah, I thought, I'm sorry I love you, too. The old 'it just happened', how many cheaters use that line? Oh, yeah, all of them. It always 'just happens', as if it were some kind of an accident, and totally out of their control. Everything just happens, except that it happens after we make a choice whether or not to allow it to happen. I've made mistakes in my life, but at least I've owned up to them.

I knew Jack wouldn't persist with the begging, and take the chance of waking the baby. I knew I'd be safe in the baby's room for hours, where I could be alone with my thoughts and my tears. I castigated myself for being so stupid as to not suspect, and for hiding in my baby's room, so that I didn't have to act out the drama that was surely coming. I grabbed a teddy bear for a pillow, and sobbed into it until it was soaked with my sorrow. I tried to calm myself down, *'Let it be.'* I tried to remember to breathe, in and out, *'Let it be'*. Then I prayed that God would send me comfort, something to calm me so that I could survive this night, and then I heard him. Not God, but John Lloyd, singing softly, *'Let it be . .'* I heard the whole song, and by the end I was asleep.

I woke up on the floor in J.D.'s room at first light, and peeked into the crib to see my sweet child's precious face still in slumber. Poor little boy had no clue about the events of the previous evening, or how they would change the course of his life. I wouldn't do to him what my Mama had done to me; make decisions based upon what I wanted for myself, rather than what was best for my child. Had I been thinking only of myself, I would have done what I always did when I was hurting, run away. But I couldn't run away any more, because I had my boy to think about; I'd have to make other living arrangements, but I wouldn't run away.

Jack was sitting on the couch when I went out into the living room, looking tired and rumpled, like he'd been sitting there all night waiting for a second chance to tell his sad, sordid story. As soon as he saw me he started the "I'm so sorry" spiel, but I put my hand up to stop him, and he stopped. I sat down across from him and I looked directly into his tired, pale-blue, watery eyes.

"Jack, I'm only going to say this once and I'm not going to argue with you, so if you're wise, you'll listen to me." I waited for him to absorb and acknowledge what I'd said, and when he did, and nodded, I continued.

"I'm going to find a place for me and the baby because this is your house, but I want you out of here until I'm prepared to move out. You will support your son, but you don't owe me anything, and I don't want anything from you.

"I will find a lawyer today, and I suggest you do the same. I don't want any explanations from you, because your excuses don't matter to me. You are who you are, and I suppose you can't help yourself.

"You told me once that your previous marriages didn't work out because you always put your career first, but that's not true. Your marriages didn't work out because you always put yourself first."

As I got up, Jack started in with his apologies, but I tuned him out and went into the kitchen to make coffee. When Jack followed me in there, I left the room, and went into the baby's room. My precious son lay there, looking up at me with the sweetest smile on his angelic face. It was all worth it, I thought, regardless of how it ended, it was all worth it.

After Jack left for the base and I put the baby down for his nap, I sat pondering how to tell my brother that he and I had both been cheated on. Just then the phone rang, and it was Will calling me to see how I was doing. Jack had already called him and confessed everything, though I didn't ask Will what that had entailed. Will told me that he was coming over, and that we would figure this out together. As I waited for him, I thought about how strangely cruel fate can be. It brings you close to a brother that you'd once lost, only to have your lives intersect in ways that cause such grief and pain. We'd lost our mother, our grandfather, John Lloyd, and now my husband, and Will's fiancée. Shelby's life seemed charmed, while mine seemed to be an exercise in futility. I don't know if I could have been so determined to find a way to make a life at that point, if not for my precious baby.

CHAPTER TWENTY~TWO

The wedding was officially off, although somehow Heather had 'misplaced' her engagement ring. Will didn't seem to care about that, telling her what she could do with it when she finally did locate it. Will mentioned to me that he'd called Shelby to tell her what had transpired, and then warned me not to call her. Will knew how tough Shelby had always been on me, and I knew he was trying to spare me more grief. Though he didn't share Shelby's thoughts on the matter, I was sure that she'd insisted that somehow this had all been *my* fault.

Sure enough, I had been right about that. I just couldn't take my brother's advice and leave well enough alone, I just *had* to call Shelby and try to explain what had happened from my perspective. I thought perhaps Will had soft-peddled it to her, but once I spoke with her I realized that she'd had the whole story. Her opinion of how I handled it, though, was what stunned me into silence.

"You know, Marra," she said, "I knew it was too good to be true! You finally have a nice, handsome, successful husband, and you go and throw him out like yesterday's trash. One little indiscretion, and you ruin not only your own life, but Will's too! You always have to ruin everything!"

My mind went totally blank, and I mumbled some lame excuse as to why I had go. The tears were streaming down my face before the phone was back in its cradle, and I berated myself for once again giving Shelby the opportunity to kick me while I was down. Maybe she's right, I thought, maybe it *was* my fault. I'd made a decision that not only affected me, but my son and brother as well.

After a good cry, it took me all of an hour to realize that Shelby was a horse's ass who didn't know what the hell she was talking about. She wouldn't have thrown Albert out and divorced him; she would have castrated him in the town square at high noon, and then she would have made mincemeat out of Heather. Who the hell was she trying to kid? It was only because it had happened to *me*, that I was supposed to swallow it. I was the second-class citizen, now, as always. I was supposed to be happy for whatever crumbs came my way because I didn't deserve anything more, unlike Shelby. She deserved only the best, as usual.

Will insisted that J.D. and I move in with him, but I wasn't going to do that. It was time to make a life for my son and me, and I didn't want to be dependent upon anyone else. I found a charming old bungalow with hardwood floors, a brick fireplace, and French doors, not far off of Main Street in Dunedin. It had a huge backyard, where Uncle Will built a custom jungle gym for Jaydee, as he called him, and where someday I'd put a pool.

Whenever Jack came to visit his son, I'd make myself scarce. Will would greet him, and sometimes even go out with him and the baby. I didn't understand how Will could forgive him for what he'd done to him, but he seemed to. More than a few times Will had tried to explain it to me, but as soon as he'd start going into detail about what Jack had told him, I'd stop him. To me it was very simple, if you're married to someone and you feel like you need to sleep with someone else, then have the common decency to sit down and tell your spouse. Jack could have whatever lifestyle he wanted, but I had the right to choose mine as well, and mine didn't include infidelity.

Jack continued his quest to apologize, and to try and win me back. He'd send me flowers, and pin letters that were filled with lame excuses on to my baby's toys. There was no excuse, as far as I was concerned. Jack had placed the blame squarely on Heather, like she was some kind of vixen who beguiled men into her lair. Men couldn't help themselves, and therefore could never be held accountable for their own actions; how ridiculous he was! He'd obviously convinced Will that it had been all Heather's fault; so much for Semper Fidelis. Up your oorah, Jack!

It was another death, although not a physical one, and it had hurt me almost as much as the others. Here I was starting my life over once again, only this time a little older and a little wiser, because now I knew that no matter what burdens still lay ahead of me, I have also been blessed.

PART V

1993, Age 39

The Power of Love

Third grade is a big deal; just ask any third-grader. You're not a baby anymore, and although your uncle might still call you by your baby name, Jaydee, and your Daddy still calls you J.D., your Mama calls you by your proper name, John Dallas. She tells you stories about an uncle you had who went to Heaven before you were born; his name was John Lloyd, almost like your name. She tells you that he is your Guardian Angel, and that he's going to watch over you so that you never have to be scared, even when the wind is blowing so hard that trees are flying by your window, and the lights go out.

It breaks your Mama's heart that you have to face death at such a tender age, but at least she knows enough by now that she can explain to you that it's not the end of life, but just another stage of it. And although we will miss the people who go on to Heaven, God will also bless our lives with new people; people whom we will love, and who will love us. And love, Mama tells her little man, never, ever dies.

CHAPTER TWENTY~THREE

Six years ago . . .

As hard as it was to be a single mother, I had to count my blessings that I had my brother nearby to help me. I also found an excellent babysitter who lived right next door, Helen Hanson. She was a sweet, older lady that J.D. called 'Ellie', and so Ellie she became to all of us. Ellie's husband, Pete, owned a candy store on Main Street, and spent most of his time there, which left Ellie bored until we moved in. She became a grandmother to my son, and was like the mother I'd never had to me. We both adored her.

Pete and Ellie had two grown daughters who'd gone to college up north and then stayed there. They also had three teenaged grandchildren that seldom came to visit, and so Ellie lavished all of her love and attention on my son, much to his delight and mine.

Ellie looked exactly like the perfect grandmother; short in stature, gray hair pulled back in a bun, cat-shaped glasses, and little black ballerina slippers. Pete was not much taller than Ellie, and wore big, square glasses on his wrinkled face. His thinning hair was combed straight back, and held in place with some kind of greasy kid's stuff. He had that old man shuffle when he walked, and although those giant glasses looked thick, he never missed a trick. J.D. called Helen 'Ellie', and Pete was 'Pop-Pop'.

Ellie and I had long conversations about life, kids, and the things that were really important. I felt as though she was a gift for me; a wise, older woman who cared enough about me to spend the time to share her wisdom. I'd been longing for someone like her in my life, without even knowing it. Ellie would always call me 'kid', and was affectionate in a maternal way that had previously been unfamiliar to me. She made me feel secure, something I hadn't felt since John Lloyd's death, and it made me worry about her, because it seemed to me that every time I'd had anyone in my life who was an anchor, they'd been taken away.

I didn't feel that way about my son, though. I worried about him the way any mother worries about her child, but I was *his* anchor, not the other way around. I was here to make him feel safe and secure, and since his father spent so little time with him, that job was mine alone.

J.D. was a good little boy who learned how to read by the time he was four. His teachers at the Methodist preschool around the corner were delighted with him, as was his doting Uncle Willie, who seemed to spend more of his free time at my place than his own. Jack had spent a minimal amount of time with our son since we'd divorced, so I wasn't totally surprised when he came by to announce that he was moving back to California so that he could spend more time with his teen-aged daughter. I wanted to remind him that instead of having one child who didn't know him, he'd now have two, but there'd be no changing his mind; Jack had always done exactly what he'd wanted to do.

I remember standing over J.D. as he slept that night, crying softly for the little boy who would grow up without a daddy, when I felt a hand on my shoulder. I turned to see who it was, but there was no one there. When I looked back at my sleeping baby, I saw John Lloyd standing over him, smiling sweetly. Then he looked up at me, and began to sing *I'll Be There*, just as if he were alive.

I knew that this was his way of telling me that he'd watch over us, that I didn't need to be afraid, and that I wasn't alone. His visits were comforting, and although I welcomed them, I secretly wondered if I was losing my grip on reality - whatever grip I'd ever had.

Jayne came to visit when J.D. was three years-old, and she was six months pregnant. She was thrilled about her pregnancy, because she'd started to believe that it would never happen. She and Dylan were both attorneys who had always put their careers first, but then Jayne's biological clock started to chime, right along with Edith's mouth, lamenting her lack of grandchildren. Poor Jayne had gone through several rounds of in-vitro fertilization before she finally achieved success.

Jayne was going to have a daughter, and delighted in hearing all about J.D.'s birth and babyhood. She'd paid more attention to him during her visit than she did to me. We went shopping, and to the beach, and most evenings Will joined us for dinner. I could have been mistaken, but I'd have sworn that she was flirting with Will during her stay. I supposed that either I was imagining that, or that pregnancy had raised her hormone level to 'insane'. I enjoyed the visit, and promised that J.D. and I would come to visit her after she delivered; and we did.

After we got back home from visiting the newborn, redheaded, blue-eyed Bridget Edith Fitzpatrick, H.B. called to tell me that his sister Luanne was selling Maybank Fine

Art & Antiques to Mr. Jason Hauser (John Lloyd's Jason). Upon cleaning out her stock room, Luanne discovered that she was in possession of some items that belonged to me; the Stickley chair, the Theus painting, and my family Bible. She'd offered to either send them to me, or buy them from me.

I'd decided to have Luanne send me the family Bible, and accepted the offer she'd made on the Stickley chair and Theus painting. The chair didn't fit my décor, and the painting, a portrait of a woman who was rather homely, was downright morbid. The cash from the sale of the two items netted me a tidy profit. It was found money, because I'd totally forgotten about my attic treasures, and had it not been for John Lloyd, I'd have pitched them out! It brought back the memories of combing through the attic with John Lloyd, and that led to all of my other memories of him. I found myself thinking of him frequently, but on days like this, it felt as though he were right there with me. There were times I'd hear him talking; I'd be questioning something in my mind, and I'd hear his answer. I'd swing around, expecting to see him standing there behind me, and find myself in tears at his absence. I would spend hours mourning the loss of my closest friend, and of not being able to feel the comfort of his arms around me.

H.B. surprised us by delivering our family Bible in person. He stayed with Will at the beach, but spent lots of time at my house getting to know J.D. It was H.B. who convinced me to start calling my son by his proper name.

178

He talked about the trials caused by going through life with initials for a name, which was why he'd called his son John Lloyd. Also, he'd said, calling my son John Dallas would pay homage to John Lloyd, and that clinched it for me.

It was during H.B.'s visit that Will told us that he'd accepted an assignment to supervise the Electronic Systems Center at Hanscom Air Force Base, twenty miles north of Boston. He'd be gone at least two years, and that made my heart sink. I'd become so dependent upon my brother for so much. Not only was he a terrific uncle to my son, but I'd be up a creek without his handyman services. He'd been the one I'd call for every little thing around the house. I was in a quandary about where I'd turn in an emergency.

As sad as I was about it, if not for Will's decision to leave town, I never would have met Alex. Well, that, and my son's decision to try to flush a dozen baby wipes down the toilet.

CHAPTER TWENTY-FOUR

Alejandro Ricardo Serrano was originally from Fajardo, Puerto Rico, but had lived in Florida for the past fifteen years. Right out of high school, he'd been drafted by the Philadelphia Phillies, whose farm team played next door in Clearwater. He played minor league ball for two years before being called up to the 'bigs'. Playing third base in his third major league game, he received a knee injury that sidelined him permanently, and had sent him into doing construction work, instead of realizing his dream of having a career in baseball.

Alex had been doing some remodeling work next door for Pete and Ellie when my toilet situation reached critical-mass proportions. At first, I didn't have a clue about what to do, or whom to call for help, and then I remembered Alex. I'd seen Alex from a distance, walking from his truck, that was parked out on our brick-paved street, to the Hanson's house, but I'd never seen him up close, or spoken with him. Ellie had raved about what a great handyman he was; she said he could fix anything. She kept inviting me over to see the work he was doing, but I was always busy with something else. After taking John Dallas to preschool, and mopping up the mess he'd made, I went next door to ask for help.

To my great surprise, Alex answered the door, and introduced himself as Ellie's friend. He was tall, dark, and handsome - like a hunky male calendar model. He had long, curly dark hair, eyes so dark brown they looked black, and stunningly-white teeth. His muscles stretched his white tee shirt in all the right places, showing ripped abs, and long, tanned arms that sported bulging biceps. He had a slight Hispanic accent, which made him even sexier.

I found myself stuttering while trying to explain my predicament. I have never before, nor since, stuttered. He stood there, grinning at me like the Cheshire cat, while I made a complete fool of myself.

"I need help, I mean, my toilet needs . . . I mean, I've overflowed . . . or not me, but my son overflowed . . . no, I mean, my son didn't overflow, he made the overflow . . . I mean he flushed them down, baby wipes . . ."

"Whoa Princess, cálmate!" Alex said, grinning from ear to ear.

I'm sure that he wasn't unfamiliar with flustered females. You can't go through life looking like him, and not upset the ladies.

"Now," he said, leering lasciviously down his straight nose at me "how can I help ju?"

"Ju? Oh, you mean me? Of course you mean me, I'm sorry. Ellie told me you could fix anything, and my brother used to fix everything for me, but he moved to Massachusetts, and now my son has overflowed my toilet and . . ." I took a deep breath and started over.

"I'm sorry; I sound like a run-on sentence. It's just that I'm a little flustered. I wasn't expecting you to answer the door, I guess. Is Ellie home?"

"Jes, she is home, but you came to have me, no?" He smiled at me, flashing his dazzling white teeth, while his gleaming, dark, sexy eyes sparkled, with brows raised suggestively above them.

"I came to have you?" I questioned. "Oh, you mean I came to *get* you!" I giggled. I actually giggled. I was mortified at myself for behaving like a teenaged schoolgirl.

"Are ju an English teacher?" Alex asked sincerely, brows knitted questioningly.

"I'm so sorry! I should just shut up now, and go away. I'm sorry," I said, as I turned, and then ran across the lawn to my front door. I had never embarrassed myself so utterly, or thoroughly, in my entire life. As I was fleeing, I could hear him yelling to me.

"Princess!" he called, "Wait up! I am coming for you! Jus' let me grab my toolbox!"

I ran inside my house, slamming the door behind me, and leaned against it while I hyperventilated. I couldn't understand what had just transpired. I was an idiot! I had never been so rude to anyone in my life. I knew perfectly well what he had been saying, yet I repeated each thing, and corrected his English! Oh, my God, what was wrong with me? I could feel my heart thumping in my chest, like it was ready to explode. Just then, Alex began pounding on my door.

"Hello? Princess?" he sang, "It is me, your knight in shining armor, here with my tools to make you happy!"

I could hear him laughing, and his deep, low chuckle made me laugh as well - he was here with his tools to make me happy! When I realized he wasn't going away I opened the door, and there we stood, grinning at one another like a couple of fools. No point in trying to pretend, I put my hands up in mock surrender.

"Okay, okay, use your tools, and make me happy!" I exclaimed.

And he did. Not that day, that would have been *way* too promiscuous for me, and out of my comfort zone, but not too long afterward. We'd danced around each other for weeks, flirting, hinting, and barely touching; that dance that couples who are desperately trying to hold out do; the dance that makes every word innuendo, every move a come-on, every touch electric. I swear, I don't know how we waited as long as we did.

Ellie wholeheartedly approved of my relationship with Alex, and John Dallas adored him. Alex taught my son how to play baseball and soccer, how to climb trees, and how to fish. They were like two kids playing together, a big one and a small one. Alex had a youthful exuberance about him that made me happy just to be near him. He saw goodness in everything around him. He loved animals, and children, and art, and music, not to mention every sport that was ever invented. We'd stroll down Main Street, and wander into every art gallery, gift shop, and antique store, and then sit outside the café and have lunch. We'd walk down to the Marina and watch dolphins and manatees at play. We'd feed the pelicans, while fishermen cast their lines for redfish and snook. We'd skate or bike on the trail when the weather wasn't too hot. It was Alex who supervised the building of the pool in my backyard, calming my nerves whenever there was a problem with one of the subcontractors.

Alex was always the encourager, and always ready for the next adventure. He was my emotional opposite;

where I was dark and depressed, he was bright and happy. I found myself hoping that Charles Reade knew what he was talking about when he wrote, *"It is said that opposite characters make a union happiest."*

I'd had a deep relationship with John Lloyd, and a comfortable relationship with Jack, but it was Alex who, for the first time in my life, brought real happiness to my heart. I was hesitant when he'd first suggested moving in with us, but he was at my house all the time anyway, and besides, John Dallas had insisted.

CHAPTER TWENTY-FIVE

I was glad that Alex was there with us that September when Hurricane Hugo hit Charleston, destroying the Maybank's beach home on Sullivan's Island, and killing Annabelle in the process. The news stung me, and brought up all of the memories that I had of John Lloyd, Papa Joe, and my years in the low country. The well of pain and sadness rose up inside of me like a vast ocean wave, taking me by surprise, and dragging me down into a trough of despair. I'd had no idea that the embers of my agony still burned so hot inside my soul. I was overwhelmed by the emotional upheaval going on inside of my brain. I suppose that I'd thought it was all behind me, but once again, death reared its ugly head, beckoning me to face it.

Alex stayed home and took care of John Dallas so that I could go to Charleston to attend Annabelle's funeral. Will flew down from Massachusetts and met me at the Francis Marion Hotel, where I'd reserved rooms for the two of us. The old hotel was oozing with Southern charm, but no one seemed to take much notice, everyone's mind was on the destruction that lay just outside its doors. I'd been ill-prepared for the devastation that had been visited upon the entire area. The losses were catastrophic - homes, businesses, and worst of all, lives.

H.B. and Missy were inconsolable at their loss of Annabelle. While she might have been a tad shallow and superficial, Annabelle had truly been one of the last surviving authentic Southern belles. Her style and manners were impeccable. Although I'd never felt any real warmth from her heart, Annabelle's words dripped like honey from a begonia, and nobody could resist her beauty and charm. My own mother had aspired to be an 'Annabelle', but she'd never had the sophistication or culture. Mama had lost the man she loved to this shallow beauty, how it must have broken her heart. I wondered if H.B. knew that Mama was pregnant when she disappeared from Charleston, and then I wondered if Annabelle had known as well.

I suddenly realized that Annabelle's death was causing me to reflect upon Mama's life. I was seeing her from a totally different perspective now – it was like I was examining her life in hindsight. The picture of who Mama had been was being colored-in with some details of her youth. A love triangle had caused her to run away with a man she didn't love; I wondered if that had been the thing that had driven him to drink. I wondered if Daddy was still alive out in the world somewhere, or if he'd gone on to meet his maker. There was so much I didn't know about the people who had brought me into the world, to me, they were virtual strangers.

There I was, back at Trinity United Methodist Church on Meeting Street in Charleston, just around the corner from where I'd once lived, and gone to school. All of the memories of John Lloyd's funeral came flooding back, and though I was sorry for what had happened to Annabelle, and to the entire area, my tears were more for myself, and for what I'd lost here years before. I suppose because I'd become so adept at suppressing my feelings, when I did allow myself to acknowledge my loss, it was overwhelming.

Will was a great support for H.B., and I was happy that he was there to comfort his father. Although I felt sorry for Missy, I found it hard to abide her strident display of grief. Her constant wailing was drowning out the pastor's words of comfort. Missy, as usual, demanded to be the center of attention. I tried to console her as best I could without rolling my eyes in the process. I might have involuntarily shushed her a few times, but she couldn't have heard anything I'd said over her own howling.

A reception was held at the Maybank's estate after the service. The mansion had escaped major damage from the terrible storm, with the exception of a few broken windows, and the felling of two big live oak trees. It had been several weeks since the storm had blasted through the area, and clean-up was still in progress. People tipped their hats as the funeral procession drove by, experiencing the feeling of mutual grief that a devastated community shares.

Will and I had very little time alone, but he'd told me that he and Jayne had met in Boston several times for dinner and drinks. I was glad that he knew somebody up there that he could socialize with. I'd been feeling a little guilty that I hadn't called him very often since meeting Alex, and I shared that with him.

Will said that he'd noticed a change in me, that I seemed content, and that contentment was something he'd never observed in me before. His comment struck an odd chord in me, because I'd been thinking the very same thing about him. Will seemed contented and relaxed, as if whatever had been bothering him his entire life had vanished. I wondered if it there was something more that he wasn't sharing, but with the pain and anguish around us, we didn't have much time to delve into many subjects other than those at hand.

We stayed in Charleston only two days, and then left in separate directions, happy to be leaving the grief and devastation behind. As my plane lifted skyward, I stared incredulously at the landscape down below that I'd been horrified by. It was hard to believe that Mother Nature could be so cruel, but seeing foundations of homes with no house standing on them, and ships piled up like toy boats in the harbor, was real proof of her catastrophic power. I was thinking about the events of earlier that day, when Will and I stood at the front steps of what had been Papa Joe's home. We'd seen the slate floor of the front foyer, the hardwood floors of the kitchen, living, dining, and bedrooms, and the tile floor of the old bathroom. That was all that was left of the house - just floors. Generations of memories had been wiped out in moments.

I thought about how John Lloyd and I had gone through the attic of that old house together, finding the keys to the secrets that had been locked up there so many years before, and how, if it hadn't been for him encouraging me up those attic stairs, just like Mama had tried to do in my dream, we would have never known . . . we would have never set up that meeting with H.B. at the beach house . . . if only . . .

Down at the marina, boats were crushed into piles, masts were bent and broken, motors were missing - and it was all sitting in the muck while the sun shone down, as if nothing had changed. And life goes on.

CHAPTER TWENTY-SIX

I was happy to return to my safe world; my son, my man, my home, and my job. Ellie had taken good care of all of them in my absence, and I don't know what I would have done without her. She was such a comfort to me, she always seemed to know what I was thinking, and would say just what I needed to hear.

When I'd told Ellie about the horrific things I'd seen in Charleston, she wrapped her arms around me, and in her raspy, ex-smoker's voice said, "Kid, erase that picture from your memory, and in its place put the angelic face of your baby boy. Life is much too short to dwell on the unhappy thoughts and sadness. You have to think about all of the good things you have, your baby, and that hunk!

Mother of God, if I had a man like that when I was your age, I'd be turning cartwheels!"

Ellie was right, I had a lot to be happy about. Alex had a way of making everything an adventure, and so I found myself doing things I'd never done before and finding great joy in them, like going to baseball games. Living in spring training paradise, we were surrounded with baseball teams - the Blue Jays here in Dunedin, the Phillies in Clearwater, and the Cardinals in St. Petersburg - and Alex would take us to see them all. By the time John Dallas started kindergarten, he knew the stats on every major league star.

Alex kept insisting that we needed to do something special for John Dallas on his first day of 'real school', kindergarten. I didn't want to take him anyplace, because I knew he'd be tired, and he had to go to school the next day. Alex had asked me if it was alright for him to give John Dallas a special gift, something he'd never forget; but when I questioned him about what he'd had in mind, he'd be vague, and say that he wasn't sure yet. He was working on something, but he didn't know if he could pull it off in time. If I'd known what he'd had in mind beforehand, I would never have allowed it, and I'm sure that's exactly why Alex had kept me in the dark.

When the pudgy yellow Labrador Retriever puppy waddled into the kitchen where John Dallas sat, having his first-day, after-school snack, my son's blue eyes got as wide as saucers, and his smile was twice that - when he realized what he was seeing.

"Mama! Look at him, I love him!" And with that, he jumped down and squealed with delight, as the chubby puppy licked his face up and down.

I shot a stern look toward Alex, who shrugged at me as if to say, *'What can ju do?'*

Alex squatted down to the puppy, and looking up, said to John Dallas, "Buddy, dare ees jus' one problem we have with dees puppy."

"What is it, Alejandro?" John Dallas said Alex's proper name in his very best Hispanic accent, rolling the r, just the way Alex had taught him.

"She ees a girl," Alex said, sadly.

John Dallas's face brightened, "Oh! That's okay! We'll just have to think of a different name!"

It dawned on me then that my innocent baby son had been conspiring with my Latin lover for quite some time. I'd been duped! We argued about names for two hours, before finally deciding that we'd just give her all three names, and so, Lola Sophia Valentina Serrano-Dallas was now an official member of our household. There was no way her full name would fit on her identity tag, so Alex got a permanent marker and wrote it on her ceramic food dish - it went all the way around the bowl.

Just as I'd heard from every mother at school, the mama becomes the primary puppy caretaker, and I was no exception. By the end of the first month, I'd felt as though I'd had another baby. There was potty training, teething, and crying in the middle of the night. Alex always offered to do it all, but he'd sleep through a hurricane, snoring loudly enough to drown out any whimpering. At first, he'd brought her into our bed, and put her between us, but that wasn't going to work; she'd wiggle around, and get up onto my head, and try to nest in my hair. Finally, we bought a puppy crate and put it alongside the bed, so that Alex could pet her through the cage when she whimpered. He'd wake up with a stiff shoulder every morning from having his arm dangling down all night, because he'd fall asleep with it in that position. Alex and John Dallas took Lola for a long walk every night after dinner, but the rest of the time she was my baby. She was lucky that she was so adorable, because after she chewed the leg of my coffee table and an expensive pair of shoes, I was ready to kill someone, and Lola was just too cute for it to be her.

Just when I was beginning to resent her, Lola matured into the most lovely, well-behaved dog I'd ever known. She was sweet, loving, gentle and kind; the perfect specimen of Labrador Retriever. She'd follow us wherever we went; there was no need for a leash, except, of course, where required by law. The most amazing thing about her was that she was bilingual! I've seen intelligent canines that seemed to understand almost everything that you'd say to them, but we had one who could *comprende en dos idiomas*. I have to admit that I was a tad jealous when Alex would call her *'mi corazón'*, meaning 'my heart'; most of the time I had no idea what he was saying to her, but that was a phrase I'd become familiar with, because he'd say it to me, although not as often as he'd say it to Lola.

Our little family was complete with the addition of our sweet dog, and it took the pressure off – John Dallas finally stopped asking for a brother!

CHAPTER TWENTY-SEVEN

In the summer of 1990, the prediction that Jack had made six years earlier regarding war in the Persian Gulf came true. Not long after, he called to tell us that he'd be leaving for Kuwait, which had been invaded by Iraqi troops. Saddam Hussein believed that Kuwait and Saudi Arabia were overproducing oil and cutting into his profits, and after the U.S. got involved, Hussein declared a 'jihad', or holy war, against the U.S. and Israel. Then, just as Jack had predicted, the proverbial shit hit the fan.

Jack sounded upbeat and excited, and I'd have sworn that he was happy about going into a war zone. He thrived on the danger and chaos of war, as if it somehow gave his life new meaning. Listening to Jack talk about the war over the phone made me recall how his face would light up, and how animated he'd become when he'd recount his military exploits. He said that he'd try to get a lay-over in Tampa so that he could say goodbye to John Dallas before shipping out, but that never happened. Typical Jack, nothing was as important as his career, and what he wanted to do.

Operation Desert Storm began in January of 1991, and by the following month there were over a half million American and allied troops deployed to the Persian Gulf. Thankfully, my brother Will was not one of them. His assignment at Hanscom had kept him busy on base, and had kept him at home.

Will had been in Massachusetts for two years, and I was excitedly anticipating his return home. Imagine my surprise when I got a call from Jayne, telling me that Will would be delaying his return to Florida for a few months so that she and three-year-old Bridget could accompany him.

I knew that Will and Jayne had become close friends, because each time I'd spoken to either of them, they'd casually mentioned that they'd seen the other; a dinner here, or a lunch there, but never did I suspect that it was anything more than a friendship. Now, I thought back on my conversations with my brother when we were in Charleston. As I had droned on about Alex, and how amazing he was, Will kept smiling at me, and nodding his head, as though he'd completely understood what it meant to be in love, and be truly happy. Now, it all made perfect sense, I hadn't been the only one who'd found love.

I'd known that Jayne had been unhappy with Dylan for years. She'd told me that she had been suspicious that he had been having an affair when she'd come down to visit me years before, but I had attributed that to her pregnant, raging hormones. I, of all people, should have known better. I had been married to a cheating dog myself. After Jayne found out that Dylan had been having affairs for years, she built a solid case against him, like any good lawyer would. It was taking some time for their divorce to be finalized because Jayne and Dylan were also in business together, and with both of them being lawyers, there was no end to the finagling that went on. Jayne didn't really need Dylan's money, because she was wealthy in her own right, but according to her, it was the principle of the thing. I would have agreed with her if she'd admitted that it was more about the *principal*, than the *principle*. She's a lawyer, money rules.

I was more interested in hearing about how Jayne had ended up with my brother, so I came right out asked her.

"After our first dinner together, Will and I decided to make it a point to get together at least once a month. We found it so easy to talk to each other, I mean, you know how your brother is, Marra! After a few drinks one night, I just came out, and confided in Will about my suspicions regarding Dylan's philandering. I broke down in tears, and Will comforted me. And, you know, one thing led to another," Jayne said.

I rolled my eyes at that one, and after a few minutes of silence I said, "This sounds like a familiar story."

"Listen, Marra, I know that this is a sore subject for you, but it's not the same at all! I'd known my marriage was over *long* before I became intimate with Will. Will is everything that Dylan is not, including a wonderful father figure for my daughter," she explained.

"I know firsthand about that," I agreed, "He's always been so fantastic with my son."

Though it took me a while to digest it all, once I got over the initial shock, I was delighted for both of them. Feeling the way I do about infidelity, it was hard for me to swallow Jayne's 'it just happened' routine, but I did believe her about Dylan's cheating. I still believed that two wrongs didn't make a right, though. She should have ended her marriage *before* getting involved with my brother. Because I loved them both, I chose to withhold judgment and wish them well. It's not easy to find happiness in life, so you have to grab it where you can, according to Ellie.

CHAPTER TWENTY-EIGHT

Will and Jayne were married on the fourth of July at the Bon Appetit restaurant on the Dunedin waterfront. The reception was held in the upstairs banquet room, which boasted walls of windows and a panoramic view of the turquoise waters of St. Joseph Sound. It wasn't the lavish affair she'd had the first time she married, but it was lovely all the same. Little four-year-old Bridget was the flower girl, although most of the flowers she tossed about ended up in her copper-colored hair, and seven-year-old John Dallas was the ring bearer. His big, blue eyes stared soberly ahead, revealing the great responsibility he felt in this important job his Uncle Willie had entrusted to him.

Shelby's girls, Darcy and Deidre, were beautiful bridesmaids in designer dresses and heels. Twenty-one-year-old Darcy was stunning, with her dark, curly hair, sultry green eyes, and curvaceous body. She had just graduated college, and was starting to think about her next step. Will had talked to her about a career in the military, but Shelby was mortified by such a prospect. Deidre, the dark-eyed, petite blonde, looked more like she was twenty than thirteen, and had a precocious personality to boot. The handwriting, as Mama used to say, was on the wall; this girl was going to give her mother a run for her money.

Jayne and Will had asked me to sing *Lovin You*, but I couldn't do it. The last time I'd sung it was at John Lloyd's memorial service, and I knew I'd never be able to sing it again. Instead, I sang Etta James's *At Last*; I thought it was appropriate for their story, especially for my brother. Edith, who sat up front next to H.B., cried throughout the song, and afterward said, "Marra, we've always felt like family, but now we actually *are* family. It seems like it was our destiny!"

Had anyone ever told me that my brother would end up marrying my childhood best friend, I'd never have believed them; but fate, destiny, or whatever you want to call it, had stepped in. Some things are just meant to be. When I thought about H.B. being Will's father, *and* John Lloyd's father, it boggled my mind. There were events in my life that seemed so disconnected, and yet somehow, simultaneously connected. My past, present, and future seemed to be coming together in the twists and turns my life had taken.

I wasn't particularly happy that Will had invited Jack, who had been married and divorced again since our split, and, thanks to his latest war, was now *Major* McNeil, but it was *his* wedding. John Dallas was happy to spend some time with his dad, but by this time, he was closer with Alex than he'd ever been with his own father. Alex, ever the gentleman, handed me off with a grin to dance with Jack, after he'd had the nerve to cut in.

"How are you, Marra Dallas?" Jack said, smiling at me, just as handsome as he'd ever been. His hair was more silver than dark now, and he had a nice, deep tan, courtesy of the desert sun, which made his gray-blue eyes look even bluer.

"I'm great, Jack, how are you?"

"Oh, I'm doing swell. My daughter's happy, my son is happy, and my favorite ex-wife isn't remarried! You look great, favorite ex-wife, really sexy," he said, as he moved in close, and tried to nibble on my neck.

I pulled away, smiling, and shaking my head, and said, "Sorry, Jack, been there, done that."

"You are the love of my life, Marra, you know that! You're never going to forgive me, are you?" he asked innocently.

"Jack, I forgave you a long time ago, but we're over. We've both moved on, at least I have, haven't you?"

"Marra, I know you've moved on, but don't you ever look back? Just for old time's sake? We had some good times, didn't we?"

"Yes, we had some good times."

"We were in love, weren't we?" he asked sweetly.

"Yes, we were," I said, "We were both in love with you."

Jack chucked at that, as if I'd been kidding. We danced for a few minutes more, and then he asked, "Don't you think you could love me again, the way you used to love me?"

"Jack, you're the father of my child, and I'll always love you for that," I stated, "but I know you well enough to know that I could never trust you, and for me, trust is essential. You know what they say, Jack?"

"What's that?" he asked.

"Semper Fi!" And with that, I spun myself around, out of his arms, and danced my way back to Alex, who was standing by the bar. I grabbed him by the lapels, and then I planted a smooch on his soft, full lips.

"Whoa! Princess! Wha' deed I do to score?" Alex asked.

"Nothing, I just love you," I said, squeezing him tightly, and breathing in his luscious scent, lime, with just a hint of coconut.

Alex grinned from ear to ear, held me close, and whispered in my ear, "Te amo con todo mi corazón." I love you with all of my heart, he'd said, and I believed him with all of mine.

Shelby, who, with a giggle, would always call Alex 'Chico', as if that were funny, was all over him on the dance floor; and this from a woman who would literally look down her nose at him. It's amazing how much she'd loosen up after a bottle or two of vino. Whenever she referred to Alex when speaking to me, she'd call him "your gardener" or "your houseboy". I knew it was a dig, but I'd always let it slide. Once, when Deidre was little, she'd called Alex 'the gardener', and I'd seen Darcy nudge her, and give her the eye. Deidre innocently looked up at her big sister and said, "What? Isn't he the gardener? That's what Mommy calls him."

My sister was a snob, but I'd always chalked it up to her feelings of inferiority. People who feel inferior have to put others down in order to build themselves up. It was either that, or she was just ignorant; or maybe it was a combination of the two. I made sure to take numerous photos of her draped all over Alex, so that I could send them to her at home. I was hoping that her husband, Albert, who never attended any of our family functions, would get a real kick out of seeing his wife embracing 'the gardener'. Maybe I'd blow it up to an eight by ten glossy. Shelby had danced with Jack earlier in the evening, but they seemed uncomfortable with one another. I knew that Jack had never cared for Shelby, he'd always said that she was selfish and shallow, it takes one to know one, I suppose. I'd always thought it odd that had Shelby tried so hard to win Jack's favor when he and I were together. It was bizarre that Shelby looked up to Jack, and down on Alex, when in reality, Jack wasn't half the man that Alex was. I suppose we all have differing standards of measure when it comes to people. To me, it's the heart of a person that matters the most, and the love and loyalty they have for others.

I watched my brother and my best friend whirling around the dance floor, faces grinning with unbridled joy. Little Bridget ran out to them, and they lifted her up between them, the three of them celebrating their first dance as a brand new family.

By nine that night, we were all crowded around the windows to watch the magnificent pyrotechnic displays from Clearwater to the south, and from Dunedin causeway to the north, all of us 'Oohing' and 'Ahhing' with each colorful explosion. It was a magical night, and I was so happy for my brother, who, *at last*, had found true love.

CHAPTER TWENTY-NINE

Will, Jayne, and Bridget were living comfortably in the condo on the causeway, but decided they'd need a bigger home, after they'd discovered that Jayne had amazingly became pregnant with my brother's first child. No in-vitro, no fertility treatments, just nature, fate, destiny, or whatever you want to call it. They'd found a house in a lovely neighborhood just a few miles down the road, but stayed in the condo while remodeling and decorating it, so that it could be, according to Edith, just perfect.

Edith insisted on staying in the new house to oversee the renovations, much to the chagrin of the individual contractors who were working there. It was very considerate of her, and conveniently for Will and Jayne, she was staying for the birth of her second grandchild as well. My brother was beside himself with joy, he had believed this day would never come, because he was, after all, just three years shy of fifty!

On Friday, March 12, 1993, the weather forecast was ominous; high winds, heavy rains, and hail. There was a huge storm approaching from the western Gulf of Mexico, heading our way with hurricane-strength winds that were expected to produce tidal surges along our coast. Will called to tell me that Jayne had gone into labor, and that they were heading over to Morton Plant Hospital on the bluffs of Clearwater Harbor. I offered to take Bridget, but Will said that she'd insisted that she must go with them. Fortunately, Edith was going along with them to take care of her little granddaughter, so that Will could stay with Jayne throughout the labor and delivery.

Alex seemed worried about the weather forecast, but I honestly thought that it was just another typical Florida storm. You'd think that I would have been a bit more concerned after experiencing the aftermath of Hugo, but our weathermen weren't calling it a hurricane, just a storm. Alex had supplies ready, including an emergency generator, in case the worst should happen, and it did. By the early morning hours of March 13th, the western gulf coast of Florida had been hammered by a super-storm, much later dubbed, 'The Storm of the Century'. It was scary to live through, with seventy-mph winds battering the trees, which caused branches to hurl themselves up against the house. The rain was coming down in squalls, sideways one way, and then it would reverse itself, and come down in the opposite direction. The awesome fury of the storm's twelve-foot tidal surge pushed the water over seawalls, swamping houses, and smashing cars and boats in its wake.

The water ran down our street like a river, and stopped just two feet short of our front door. Alex had run over to Pete and Ellie's a few times during the early evening to check on the old couple. He'd tried to persuade them to come over to our house so that he could better protect them in an emergency, but they stubbornly refused to leave the comfort of their own home. They insisted that they'd lived through worse, and that they were going to bed early, and they'd see us tomorrow. During the night, Alex, John Dallas, and even Lola, slept like logs. I'd always said that Alex could sleep through a hurricane, and now I was finding that extremely annoying, because I felt as though I had to stand watch. Every hour or so I'd peek into my son's room to check on him, and I'd see John Lloyd standing over him, smiling that same charming smile he'd always had on his sweet face. The last time I looked, I could have sworn I'd seen an old woman standing next to John Lloyd, but I attributed that to fatigue.

Alex was awake by 6 a.m., and after he had his coffee, and surveyed the outside of our house, he went next door to check on Pete and Ellie. I'd been worrying

Marra Dallas

about them all night, and was anxious to hear that they were alright. Alex was back inside of twenty minutes, and I could tell by the troubled look on his face, that something was *very* wrong. He struggled to find the right words to give me the bad news, that he'd found a distraught Pete, cradling Ellie's lifeless body. She'd apparently suffered a heart attack during the night. Her body was cold when Pete found her in the morning, laying on the couch with a Carl Hiaasen novel in her lap, and a smile on her face. Ellie had enjoyed life right to the very end, doing the things that made her happy, just as she'd encouraged me to do.

Alex held me while I sobbed for Ellie, my heart was breaking over the loss of her for all of us. After all of the catastrophes I'd experienced in my life, you would think that Ellie's death wouldn't have hit me so hard, but it did. I was devastated and angry. It just wasn't fair, not to Ellie, who'd had such a zest for life, and certainly not to Pete, whose entire life centered around her. The poor man would be despondent without her. I don't know what I would have done without Alex, I just couldn't bear any more grief on my own. Alex went back over to help Pete with the arrangements, and stayed with him until Pete's brother got there to take over.

My brother's only child, Hugh Barrett Dunne, was born early that morning, though the joy of his birth was mitigated by the sorrow of Ellie's sudden death. We stayed focused on baby Barrett's birth for John Dallas's sake, and withheld the ominous news of Ellie's demise as long as possible.

John Dallas stayed with Edith and Bridget at the new house, while Alex and I went to visit Pete, who berated himself for not heeding Alex's advice to stay with us. We tried to explain to him that her heart would have given out wherever she was, but no matter what we said, Pete was inconsolable, and blaming himself for Ellie's death. As Alex sat with Pete, trying to reassure him that he'd done the best he possibly could have, I remembered that last time I had checked in John Dallas's room in the wee hours of the morning. The memory of the woman I'd seen standing next to John Lloyd, came back to my mind. It had been Ellie, standing there with John Lloyd, watching over my little boy. That was clear to me now.

I smiled as I recalled John Dallas's shining face as he recounted his first day of third grade. He loved his teachers, his friends, and his school. The only drawback for him, was that Lola wasn't allowed to go to school with him. But his loyal pet had welcomed him home with kisses and whines, as if she hadn't seen him for years, instead of just a few hours. I was so proud of him, and the way he'd handled Ellie's death. He'd cried, of course, but then smiled when he asked me if he now had two guardian angels, instead of just one. "Yes, my son," I'd said, "Yes you do." As many times as I'd had to deal with death in my life, this was so heartbreaking; to see this little lamb of mine suffering with the loss of someone he loved.

His pain over losing Ellie hurt me more than my own did. Thankfully, we had baby Barrett to soften the blow. He was an adorable little guy, with a head full of blonde curls, and those piercing robin's-egg-blue eyes, that were just like my brother's, just like John Lloyd's, and just like their father's before them. H.B. was on his way to meet his newest grandchild, and only grandson. Missy had only had one daughter, who was just as contrary and whiny as her mother.

John Dallas now knew the heartbreak of death, and the joy of birth, learned all in one day. The cycle of life, I'd told him, the way it is supposed to be. Love is born, but never, ever dies. The love that we've received from others lives on inside of our hearts, and it's never lost. And my son accepted the facts of life and death, simply because I'd told him so. It may be said that he was able to do so because of the security that my love offered him, but it was *his* love that gave me the wisdom to see the good in all of it.

PART VI

1999, Age 45

Trials, Tribulations & Truth

I sat alone in a small chapel, in an unfamiliar hospital, speaking silently to whomever cared to listen, God, John Lloyd, Ellie, Mama, Papa Joe, and my never-born baby. I was asking for mercy and healing for those whom I loved, who, at that very moment, were undergoing procedures in this building.

I was alone with my thoughts, there was no one to hold me, or tell me that everything was going to be alright. There was nobody to comfort me, or prop me up, there was only me, and the spirits of those who have departed this world before me. You would think that I'd be a religious person with all of the praying I do, but I'm not. I'd asked John Lloyd once why, if religion was so wonderful, there were so many angry religious people. He'd said that angry religious people were religious because they knew the gospel, but they were angry because they didn't know God. Religion had never brought me comfort, but my spirits had, and I believed they were from God. When I'm inconsolable, they reassure me. One in particular even serenades me with a song, that will speak to my heart, and bring me comfort. He'd promised me that he'd be there *'like a bridge over troubled water'*; it is ironic that his life here ended on a bridge.

I heard the door open behind me, and turned to see a large man in scrubs, peering into the darkness of the tiny chapel. When his eyes adjusted to the light, he motioned for me to join him outside in the hallway. I rose slowly, and made my way along the aisle to the heavy door that lead to the news, good or bad, and to the inevitable events that the future will hold, shaped by the crux of that news. 'I am ready', I told my spirit friends, 'if you are', and I pushed the heavy door open, and ventured out, into the blinding brightness.

CHAPTER THIRTY

Five years earlier . . .

Alex's business was so busy that he had to hire five guys to help him with all of the work he had. I, on the other hand, had the opposite problem. I had only been assigned one evening class that met on Tuesday and Thursday nights, leaving me with plenty of leisure time. Alex was talented at whatever work he did, drywall, painting, plumbing, tile, and stonework, but he wasn't a businessman. Thus began my illustrious career with *'The Home Run Handyman'*. I became Alex's office manager, a catch-all for accounting, payroll, secretarial, billing, and whatever else had to be done in the office to keep the business running. It made Alex happy, and helped to assuage his angst over the baseball strike. A year without a World Series was tantamount to torture for him.

It was a perfect fit, and I found that I really enjoyed working from home with my faithful pet by my side. Lola would lie on my foot while I sat at the desk, so that she could comfortably doze; if I so much as made a move to go anywhere, she'd know about it. God forbid I sneak off for a snack, and she not share it!

I'd never thought of myself as a particularly jealous person, even after what I'd gone through with Jack, but there were times when women would call, and insist on speaking personally with Alex, that I could feel my blood boiling. Maybe it was because I was approaching forty, or because I had found my first gray hair, or that I'd noticed that my smile lines didn't disappear when I stopped smiling; whatever it was, jealousy had reared its ugly head. It was the year that Lorena Bobbitt had brought revenge to a whole new level, so I taped a picture of her up on my refrigerator as a subtle reminder to Alex of what could happen if he strayed. He thought it was comical, covered his 'man jewels' protectively and said, "I only have eyes for ju, Princess! Te quiero a ti, y sólo a ti." Damn, he was cute. '

Working from home also gave me more time for my favorite pastime, reading. I was still a voracious and eclectic reader, devouring Stephen King, Rosamunde Pilcher, Ken Follett, Michael Connelly, and E.M. Forster, all in the same month. The cordless phone allowed me to lay by the pool and read a book without missing a call. It was a tough job, but somebody had to do it. Working from home also allowed me to watch the entire real-life courtroom drama of the OJ Simpson murder trial. I decided that I'd use it as a course study of our legal system, and maybe teach a class on it one day. It was also of great interest to me personally, because of my own history. I saw similarities between Nicole and my mother; they had both become enamored with a man who was powerful, charismatic, and sadistic. They had hidden the abusive relationship that they had found themselves in, because of embarrassment and pride, and then left themselves in a dangerous situation for far too long.

After nine long months of damning testimony, the ridiculous people serving as jurors returned a 'not-guilty' verdict in only four hours. It served to reinforce my belief that people will always do what's in their own best interest, even if it's not the right, or fair thing to do. To me, hearing that verdict vindicated my own actions of bringing justice to my mother's killer. I felt sorry for Nicole and Ron's family members, because they hadn't had that same opportunity. As much anger as I still carried in my heart toward Rocco Marcucci for what he had done to Mama, and for what he had stolen from me, I was relieved that he hadn't lived to get away with her murder, as OJ had with his victims. Knowing how crooked and connected the Marcucci family was in my hometown, there was no doubt in my mind, that had Rocco gone on trial for Mama's murder, he, too, would have walked away a free man.

The OJ trial caused me to realize that revealing my past to Alex was long overdue. I hadn't consciously kept it from him, but it never seemed to be the right time to tell him my story. I feared that he wouldn't understand, and think me a terrible person; though in my experience, Alex had never been harsh, or judgmental. I'd thought that I'd totally trusted him, but obviously, my holding back the truth proved that I didn't. The only person I'd ever *really* trusted was John Lloyd, and I knew that if he'd been here, he'd tell me to open up to Alex.

I started with an apology, and said that I knew that I should have told him everything sooner. I'd killed a man, a scumbag of a man, but a man nonetheless, and it wasn't an easy thing to admit. I was amazed at how casually he accepted my story.

"Alex, do you think I'm a horrible person?"

"Corazón, you could never be horrible. Things happen in life, and we do what we think is best at the time. You were a frightened child, and you reacted the only way you knew, you tried to save your Mamá, sí?"

"Sí!"

"You know, Marra, when I was a boy, my dream was to have my Papí see me play ball as a major league player, but he died before that happened. I didn't give up my dream because of that disappointment. When I was hurt, and my career as a ballplayer was over, it wasn't the end of the world, just a different path. Life happens the way it's supposed to – maybe if I'd been a big star, I would never have met jú – and that would have been tragic."

Sometimes I wondered if God's giving me Alex was his way of trying to make up for all of the pain and heartache he'd allowed into my life. Alex was the balm for my tattered soul. He was the only person who could make me forget that I'd ever felt pain, or unhappiness, or sorrow. I'd never met his mother, but I blessed her daily; she must be a sweet, kind, and loving person for having raised such a wonderful son.

CHAPTER THIRTY-ONE

My niece Darcy hadn't chosen a career in the military like her Uncle Will, but she did decide to work for the government. Her degree was in Political Science, she was fluent in Spanish, and she had a black belt in karate, so she was easily accepted into the FBI academy in Quantico, Virginia, where she passed every class with flying colors. The Bureau had been actively recruiting young women, and Darcy was among the best and brightest.

Darcy was trained as a counterterrorism specialist, because the Bureau had decided that it would be a good fit for her. On April 19, 1995, Darcy's first big assignment took her to Oklahoma City, where 168 people had been murdered when terrorists blew up the Alfred P. Murrah

Federal Building, nineteen of them being children. My niece was never the same again; her sparkle of youth, quick smile, and innocence disappeared. Darcy's bright personality darkened, like a veil had been cloaked over her. At only twenty-four, Darcy now wore the mantle of grief, to me a visible thing. Grief was something I'd been familiar with for most of my life, and I was sorry for her, it's not an easy burden to bear.

Shelby didn't understand Darcy's grief, and urged her not to dwell on it; what's past is past, just forget about it all. I knew that Darcy would eventually find happiness in life, but she would never be completely without sorrow, and would find it hard to trust. I knew these things from my own first-hand experience. Some people skate through life unscathed by tragedy, while others lives are wrought with heartbreak. Fate can be unkind and unfair.

In the late fall of 1995, Shelby and Deidre came for a visit and stayed with Will and Jayne, ostensibly because they had the bigger house. We'd gotten together a few times during their visit, taking all of the kids to the beach on Caladesi Island, to the Marine Science Center, and on Captain Memo's Pirate Cruise. Little Barrett was in the midst of the terrible twos, and wreaked havoc wherever we went. Although his sister and two cousins tried to cajole him constantly, it seemed as though none of us could keep Barrett happy. Jayne finally realized that the baby had a tooth coming in, and once she'd give him ice, or ice cream, he was happy as a clam.

The night before Shelby and Deidre left, they came over to visit with Will, Jayne, and the kids. While Will and Alex were outside on the jungle gym with the kids, I made the mistake of commenting on the outcome of OJ's murder trial in front of Deidre. Shelby shot me a warning look that made it clear that it wasn't a topic she cared to discuss in front of her daughter. Jayne caught the look as well, and when they guys came back inside with the kids, she suggested that they all go out for an ice cream, and let Shelby and I have some time alone. Leave it to Jayne, she was always trying to bring the family together. I suppose because she'd been an only child, she'd developed this romantic notion that with families, bigger was better. After the others left, I seized the opportunity to have a conversation with my sister.

"Shelby, I caught your look of disapproval, don't you think that Deidre is aware of the OJ Simpson trial? I mean, even if she doesn't watch Court TV, it's on the news and in the paper every day. She's sixteen already, and they're probably talking about it in school."

"Marra, my *disapproval*, as you call it, is not about OJ, it's about you! Deidre doesn't know about you, and I'd like to keep it that way."

"What do you mean *about me*? What do *I* have to do with the OJ trial?" I really wasn't following her line of thinking. She'd gotten upset when I'd mentioned the OJ trial, and now somehow it was about *me*?

"She doesn't know that her aunt is a murderer!" she shouted, suddenly flushed with anger. "Do you think that I want her to know about that? It's bad enough that Darcy had to find out when she went to work for the FBI!"

It took me several minutes to absorb what she'd said, I was just incredulous. I sat down across from her and stared, and my mouth was open, but I was unable to speak.

"What, Marra? Are you mad at me because I'm trying to protect my daughter?" she shrieked. This was as outwardly confrontational as she'd ever been with me. Usually, Shelby's distain was couched in civility, but not this time. She was, as Mama used to say, 'loaded for bear'.

It took me a few moments to gather my thoughts, so that I could respond. I had no idea from where this outburst had come, but obviously, it had been brewing for a long time. Could this be where the animosity I'd always felt from my sister had stemmed? It seemed preposterous.

"Shelby, are you mad at me because I tried to protect our mother, or are you mad at me because I protected myself? I mean, if he murdered Mama, do you honestly think he would have thought twice about murdering me as well? Do you think that I had any choice? If it had been him or me, would you have preferred that I just let him kill me too?"

Now, Shelby looked shocked, and uncomfortable. I don't think that she'd expected me to have a reasonable explanation for my actions. I still couldn't believe that for all these years, she'd considered me a *murderer*. When she didn't reply, I went on, "And you believe that *I'm* a murderer? Is that what you think of me? Is that why you've been so distant all these years? Were you *afraid* of me?"

She laughed then, and said, "No, Marra, I was never *afraid* of you!"

"What, then? If you weren't afraid of me, what was it that caused you to keep your distance all these years?" I demanded.

Shelby didn't respond, she just sat there, looking away from me, one leg crossed over the other, and swinging wildly. It was the same agitated response Mama used to display when she was upset.

"What *was* it then, Shelby?" I demanded, now at a emphatic volume that matched her own. For once in my life, I was *not* thinking about trying to curry favor with her. I was upset and angry, and I wasn't about to back down.

Looking down at the floor, she said, "I was embarrassed, okay?" Then she looked up at me and said, "I was embarrassed of **you**."

Stunned into silence, my mind raced to put those words into perspective. Suddenly, there was a lump burning in my throat, but I wouldn't allow myself to cry in front of Shelby. I shot up, and ran out the door. Lola followed, her tail wagging at the prospect of going for a walk. My tears began to fall in earnest as soon as I hit the street. I couldn't go far, because the dog wasn't leashed, but I had to get away from the house, and away from my sister. In all of the years that I'd tried to forge a relationship with her, I'd believed that Shelby was just aloof. She'd never had any really close friends, so I'd assumed that she was unable to open up to anyone, and I tried not to take her rejection personally; but now I'd discovered that she'd always been embarrassed of me, and *that* was personal.

I thought about going back to the house and confronting her, telling her that had she been the one to walk in on the scene I'd walked in on, she'd be dead. Shelby certainly wouldn't have acted, she'd have tried to run away. She'd always had her own best interest at heart. She hadn't kept my past a secret from Deidre because she was worried about how it would affect her child, she kept it from her because she cared about how it made *her* look. She'd probably spun some kind of fairy tale childhood stories for her kids, where she played the part of perfect child, no doubt. I wondered where I had fit in those tales, or if I'd had a role at all. Maybe the stories she told her children didn't include me, or Will, or anyone else but her, or maybe she'd never told them anything at all about her childhood, as if she'd been born this perfect adult that she'd always aspired to be.

Although we were never close, I'd foolishly believed that as the years went by, we'd forge some kind of sisterly relationship, but the truth was that we had never had any kind of relationship, because we weren't able to relate. The truth was that I'd forged a relationship with her children, but never with her. Now, it was all beginning to make some sense to me, her distance, her reticence, her contentiousness. It all came from her unresolved anger toward me. She saw me, not Marcucci, as the person who'd disrupted her life. She could have lived with her mother being murdered, because it would only have garnered sympathy for her, but her sister being a murderer reflected poorly upon her social standing.

I waited a while before returning to the house, and fortunately, by then, the others had come back, and didn't seem to notice that Shelby and I were avoiding one another like the plague, or at least they didn't let on if they did. The kids were excitedly telling stories about a monkey they'd seen at the ice cream shop, and how Barrett had tried to feed the chimp his ice cream cone. I could see Alex observing me from across the room, and when I looked at him directly, he winked and smiled. He knew I was upset, he could always read me. Later, after they'd all left, and we were lying in bed, Alex simply asked if I was ready to talk about it, and I'd told him, "Not yet."

Jayne called me the next day, after Will had gone to take Shelby and Deidre to the airport.

"Marra, is it my imagination, or is there a new layer of ice between the Dunne sisters?"

"Jayne, you know very well that I'm not a Dunne, I'm a Dallas."

"I'll take that as a yes, then. What happened, Marra?"

I told Jayne the whole story, and after she calmed down, she told me that neither she, nor Edith, had ever liked, or trusted, Shelby. I knew that Jayne never cared for Shelby, but Edith's feelings had come as a surprise, because Edith had always been so cordial with my sister. I thought about the two of them, strolling about the gardens of the Maybank estate, smoking cigarettes, and admiring the scenery. I wondered, if perhaps, Shelby had said something back then that had revealed her true nature to Edith.

I never shared any of what had transpired that night between my sister and me with my brother Will, but I'm sure that Jayne had. He'd never said anything, but he never really mentioned her much after that. Shelby's visits were infrequent, so I really wouldn't have to deal with her very much anyway. I figured that I could be cordial with her for short periods of time, if need be.

CHAPTER THIRTY-TWO

John Dallas was becoming a Little League star, with Alex's help. My son's whole life revolved around baseball now, but it hadn't always. When he'd been about ten, John Dallas went through a military faze, where he was enamored with anything to do with any branch of the service, especially the Marines. He was obviously trying to garner his father's attention, not that it did any good. It just goes to show you, even though he'd had a lot of male attention from both Alex and Will, he still craved his dad's approval. He might have seen how crazy Will was over having a son, and that had made him question how his own father felt about him. Whatever it was, it was not bringing Jack any closer, no matter how many times I'd try to explain to the idiot that he needed to show more of an interest in his boy. Whenever Jack was around John Dallas, he seemed tough, and critical of him. Perhaps in his mind, he believed that was the best way to toughen him up, but you can't do that with a sensitive child, it only hurts his feelings.

Will saw what was happening, and took the initiative to nurture John Dallas's interest. He brought him over to MacDill Air Force Base, and gave him the grand tour, took him to see the Flying Thunderbirds perform, and even took him up in a jet. It seemed to satisfy John Dallas's quest temporarily, but when asked what he wanted to be when he grew up, he'd still say a Marine. By the time he became a teenager, he was back to wanting to be a professional baseball player. It helped that the Yankees had built Legend's Field over in Tampa, where Alex had taken John Dallas for spring training, and that we were soon getting our own major league team, the Tampa Bay Devil Rays. I noticed that little by little, the Marine memorabilia was being replaced by all things related to baseball.

Alex had never tried to replace Jack as John Dallas's father, but he was certainly the best male role model a boy could ask for. He was a hard worker, had a healthy respect for women, loved all sports, and was always ready to play with John Dallas and his friends. Sometimes, I'd see Alex gliding down the street on a skateboard in the midst of four or five young teenage boys, and I'd hear one of John Dallas's friends say, *"Hey, dude, you're dad is cool!"* John Dallas would never correct them and say that Alex wasn't his dad, instead he'd say, *"Yeah, he is."* Alex had coached every Little League team that John Dallas had ever played on, and was being courted by the high school baseball coach as an assistant; just in time to coach my son at school as well.

Though I was appreciative that my son had Alex and my brother Will to make up for his father's absence, I knew first-hand that having a good relationship with one person, doesn't necessarily make up for not having a good relationship with another. I had a great relationship with Jayne, who had always been like a sister to me, but I still had that empty place in my heart that had always been reserved for my real sister.

Shelby hadn't been back to visit in over two years, not since she and I had it out. We sent one another cards for birthdays and holidays, and spoke briefly on the phone, but never about anything personal. Now, I was just as aloof toward her as she'd always been toward me, and it made me realize that I'd always been the one who had pursued a relationship with her. I felt bad about the strain between us, but I had to admit to myself that there had never really been a close relationship to begin with - that had just been my delusional imagination.

I hadn't seen Darcy or Deidre during that time either, but that was because Darcy was working in the

FBI's San Diego field office, and Deidre was at the University of Texas in Austin. The girls were good about keeping in touch, and kept promising to come and visit, but I knew it wasn't easy for Darcy to get away from her job for any length of time, and Deidre was, after all, a college coed. I'm sure she didn't want to spend her spring break with a bunch of old people and little kids.

Early one summer morning, Jayne called to ask me to come by for a visit, saying she had something she wanted to talk to me about. She was a tad mysterious about the subject matter, but I tried not to read anything into that. I thought maybe she was just lonely, with Will being on an assignment in Birmingham, and the kids being in New Jersey visiting Edith. Bridget and Barrett had flown up with H.B., who had come down here specifically to fly up with them to visit their grandmother - whom he'd been romancing for quite some time.

Jayne was sitting out by the pool, reading a book, and sipping a tropical drink, when I got there. She offered to make me one, but I've never been much of a drinker, especially in the morning.

"So, do you think your mother and Will's father are serious?" I asked.

"She just told me yesterday that they love each other!" Jayne exclaimed.

I raised my eyebrows, "You think they're *doing it*?"

"Please!" Jayne yelled, spitting her drink out, "They're *old!*"

"Hey, old people do it too!"

"Ugh! That's just nauseating to think about," Jayne uttered disgustedly.

"So, what did you want to talk to me about?" I asked her, changing the subject, and hopefully, the mental picture of her mother and H.B. that she'd conjured up.

"Shelby called . . . there's no easy way to say this, so I'm just going to tell you straight out. Shelby was diagnosed with breast cancer," she said, and when she saw the look on my face, she leaned over and patted my hand as she added, "I'm so sorry, Marra."

"When?" I asked.

"She called last night, but I don't know how long she's known. You know Shelby, she's always short on details. She's scheduled for surgery next week, and I told her that we'd come, is that okay?" she asked, and I nodded. Then she added, "I called my mom, and told her we're coming. Will Alex take care of John Dallas, or do you want to bring him?"

"Alex will take care of him. It's not something that I'd want him there for, you know?"

We made our plans, and flew out that Sunday morning. Jayne rented a car in Newark, and we drove up to Edith's home in Smoke Rise. After visiting with Edith, H.B. (who, by the way, looked awfully cozy in Edith's home), and Bridget and Barrett, we got back into the rental and headed to Shelby's house.

Shelby and Albert lived a few miles away in North Caldwell, in a house that could be called a mini-mansion. It echoed Shelby's personal style, well manicured and aesthetically magnificent. Albert was seldom at home, as he spent most of his time in Manhattan, where his office was located. Often, he'd grab a helicopter into the city from the nearby airport, the same one that John F. Kennedy Jr. occasionally flew out of; the same airport where John Jr. would take his last fateful trip later that same summer.

Shelby embraced me when we arrived, and thanked me for coming. In that instant, all of the hard feelings I'd had toward her melted away, and I filled with compassion for her because of the ordeal she was facing. Neither Jayne nor I had been to Shelby's home in many years, so we were given the grand tour by our hostess.

The house was a showplace, but there was no warmth, it was cold and austere. I whispered to Jayne that I couldn't imagine why two people would need all of that space, not to mention a butler's pantry. "They don't have a butler, do they?" I'd facetiously asked Jayne. Not getting my attempt at humor, she quietly explained to me that it was just a pantry, no butler was required. I pretended to be shocked by that fact, which tickled Jayne, as I'd known it would. I *'oohed'* and *'aahed'* appropriately in each room, as was expected of me, but I was unimpressed. I'd expected Shelby's house to be a showplace, with museum quality appointments. Jayne appreciated the décor, and used terms like balustrade, pediments, and cabriole. Terminology I was familiar with when it related to European architecture, but certainly seemed pretentious when describing home décor. These were the things that made Shelby happy, God only knew why.

Shelby seemed like her old self during the tour, but I suppose that was because she was in her element, and wasn't thinking about anything else, like tumors and surgery. When we returned to the kitchen, Shelby said, "Of course you'll be staying here with me," as if that fact had already been established. Jayne and I looked at each other, uncertain of what to say. Jayne took the lead.

"Well, Shelby, we didn't want you to have to entertain, and you certainly need your rest tonight, so we thought we'd stay at Mother's."

"Oh, well, I had Gloria make up two rooms for you already, it's really no trouble at all," Shelby countered.

I looked at her and saw, for the first time, the fear in her eyes. I was tired of the game she was playing, pretending that everything was alright, so I came to the point.

"Shelby, do you want us to stay here with you?" I asked.

"Well I thought, you know, that since Edith had the children anyway, that, you know, you girls would be more comfortable here."

She was pussy-footing around, as usual. Shelby just couldn't bring herself to admit that she needed anyone, or anything. She was the most prideful person I'd ever known. I had to wonder how her husband dealt with her on a regular basis.

"Where's Albert?" I asked, suddenly taking another tack.

Shelby's eyes widened in surprise at the question, and then she shrugged. "He usually stays in the city during the week. He's got to be in the office early, and usually works late, and the commute is awful!"

I was tempted to ask about the helicopter, but I bit my tongue. Something was amiss here, but Shelby wasn't going to admit it. I mean, if your wife is on the cusp of major surgery, would your very first concern be about commuting? I'd always thought that Albert was a cold fish, but this was ridiculous! Something just didn't sit right with me about Shelby's explanation of Albert's absence.

Under the circumstances, I thought it was best to go easy on Shelby in all things, so I let my curiosity wane. I'd deal with Albert at a more convenient time.

"I'd love to stay here with you," I said, then turned to Jayne and asked, "Maybe you want to go back to Edith's, and help her with the kids?" I wasn't actually sure what Jayne wanted to do, but I was giving her an out, just in case.

"No, no! I'd much rather stay here with you two," Jayne said. "I'll just need to call my mom, and let her know."

"I'll go out to the car and get our bags," I said, and leaned over to give Shelby a hug - just as she turned away from me, and guided Jayne to where the phone was.

Although Shelby had been to Sloan Kettering for a second opinion, she'd opted for a local surgeon, who'd been recommended by her own oncologist, as well as by the doctor she saw at Sloan. Her surgery was scheduled for early the next morning at her local hospital. She told us that she'd ordered a car to come for her at 5 a.m., and that we should sleep in, and come up to the hospital later.

"Are you crazy?" I asked Shelby.

"What do you mean, Marra? Crazy about what?"

"We're not letting you go by yourself in a hired car with a stranger! We're taking you!" I scolded.

"Marra," Shelby said sternly, "that is absolutely unnecessary! There's no point in the two of you hanging around the hospital all day. I'll be anesthetized, I won't know if you're there or not!"

That was Shelby, always the voice of reason, no feeling, but plenty of reason. She was absent-mindedly filing her perfectly manicured nails, so as to have a good reason not to make eye contact with anyone.

"You'll know that we're with you in the car on the way there, and you'll know that we're with you when you get prepped, and you'll know that we're there with you right before the surgery," I said, "And you'll know that we're there with you when you wake up." I could feel myself tearing up, but Shelby didn't bat an eye; rather, she sighed, as if I were being childish.

"Oh, all right Marra! I swear, you make such a federal case out of everything!" Shelby replied.

That night, after Shelby went to bed, Jayne and I sat on a balcony outside of my room.

"Jaynie, I think she's in denial."

Jayne sighed, "I know, Marra, but I think it's easier for her if she pretends it's no big deal."

"But don't you think that's dangerous?" I asked. "I mean, sooner or later, it's going to hit her. And where the hell is that prick she's married to?"

"I know! Can you believe it? I'm not buying that commuting story for one minute. Charlie worked in the city, and came home to Mother and me every single night," Jayne added. We talked for another hour, and then went to bed, setting our alarms for 4 a.m. so Shelby couldn't try and sneak off without us.

Jayne and I sat in the O.R. waiting room with a slew of other tired family members. Little kids were whining, and men were pacing, and I felt like I couldn't breathe. I looked over at Jayne, and she looked as claustrophobic as I felt, so I suggested we go for a walk. Once outside of the hospital, Jayne turned her cell phone on.

"Uh oh, Edith's called already! She can't stand not knowing what's going on. Let me just give her a quick call."

I meandered down the sidewalk while Jayne spoke with her mother on the phone. I could hear her raising her voice a few times, and then I heard her tell her mother not to worry. I couldn't imagine what that was all about, except maybe that the children were too much for her. Edith was aging gracefully, still a lovely looking woman in her late sixties, but young kids are a handful for the young, never mind those who are aged. I heard Jayne's heels clicking hurriedly toward me.

"Marra!" Jayne shrieked.

I turned, and saw the distraught look on her face.

"What is it?" I asked.

"It's H.B.! He's had a heart attack! He's on his way here in an ambulance, and Mother wants me to come home to stay with the kids, so that she can come here and be with him."

"Oh, my God! Is he going to be okay?" I felt my heart sink, it was insult to injury. Here we were worrying about Shelby, and now H.B. was in distress.

"She thinks so. She said that the paramedics said he was stable, but he needed to come to the hospital for an angiogram. They think it's a blockage."

"Okay, you go. I'll stay here and wait for H.B., and then for Edith. They should be settled in before Shelby's out of surgery."

Jayne hugged me to herself, "Oh, Marra, I'm so sorry. I feel like I'm abandoning you."

"It's okay, honey, you go, and hurry up! I'm sure Edith wants to be here."

I found my way to the ER just in time to see H.B. being wheeled in, and I ran to his side. Other than being pale, he looked pretty good. His face lit up when he saw me, and it was obvious to me, in that moment, that he genuinely cared for me.

"Marra, darlin', you're a sight for sore eyes."

"H.B., how are you feeling?"

"Good, darlin', Ah'll be right as rain. Now you go off to your sister, ya hear? Don't worry about me, child."

I gave him a hug, and told him I loved him, and then offered to stay with him while he went through his procedure.

Holding on to both of my hands, and looking at me with such adoration, he said, "Marra, darlin', y'all have been like a daughter to me. I can see why John Lloyd loved you like he did, just like I loved your mama before you. Y'all are such a good girl, Marra. Never have you asked me about me and your mama, even after you knew I was Will's daddy.

"I just want y'all to know that I did not know that your mama was pregnant when I broke it off with her. I was wrong, darlin', I should've fought for her, but I let my daddy control me back then, and I married Annabelle, like he wanted me to. It wasn't until after I was married, that I'd heard that Charlotte had been sent off to the unwed mother's home. I threw a fit with my daddy, but it was too late, he'd told me, I'd already made a vow to Annabelle. I'm sorry, Marra."

The tears were flowing freely down my face as H.B. held onto my hands, and confessed his love for Mama. The questions I'd always had about whether or not he'd known about Mama being pregnant with Will, were finally answered. Both H.B and Mama had been the victims of the social pressures of their day.

"It's okay, H.B., you did what you thought was the right thing at the time, I understand. Don't we all look to the people we love for acceptance and approval, even if it hurts us?"

He smiled weakly, and stroked my cheek, "Darlin' Marra, you are a treasure, a beautiful treasure. Please tell Miss Edith that I love her, would y'all do that for me?"

"You'll be able to do that yourself, as soon as you're out of surgery! You'll be fine, I just know you will!' I said, but in my mind, I was praying that my words would ring true, and that I would get to say 'I told you so' to him, soon afterwards.

The nurse came to take H.B. away, and shooed me out the door. I hurried back upstairs to check with the nurse at the desk, and was told that Shelby was still in surgery. She promised me that the doctor would come and find me as soon as it was over. I couldn't believe that Albert hadn't showed up, but there was always the possibility, knowing Shelby, that she hadn't told him. After all, she hadn't told her daughters; insisting that there was no point in *'disrupting their lives over a procedure whose outcome wouldn't be affected one way or the other by whether or not they were in attendance'.*

I couldn't face going back into that waiting room with all of those pasty-looking people, so I wandered the halls until I saw a sign for the chapel. I peeked inside, and saw that there was only one person, a man, sitting up front alone, so I took a seat in the back. With my head bowed, and my eyes closed, I suddenly heard the sweet voice of John Lloyd singing *Amazing Grace,* and peeked up to see if the man who'd been sitting up front could hear him too, but there was no one there; I was alone in the chapel. As John Lloyd sang, I prayed, until the singing ceased, and the large man in the scrubs opened the door of the small, dark chapel, letting the brightness from the outside world spill into the dark sanctuary.

He beckoned me out, and I gathered myself up, and headed toward the unknown, chin up, ready to take the hit that I knew was surely headed my way.

CHAPTER THIRTY-THREE

The doctor's news was good, Shelby's surgery had gone well, a minor lumpectomy, and her margins had all been clear. As the doctor exited down the hallway, I turned around, and walked away, down the hall, and back to the nurse's station. I asked when my sister would be out of recovery and in a room, and was told it would be an hour or two, so I went in search of Edith to tell her Shelby's good news.

I didn't know why I'd gotten so spooked in the chapel. Seeing or hearing John Lloyd *usually* brought me a feeling of well-being, and so I'd been so sure that Shelby's doctors were going to give me horrible news. I should have felt relief, but that dark cloud was still hanging over my head. I hoped that it wasn't a bad omen about H.B., but from what Edith had told me, it sounded as though it should be a simple procedure, and easy recovery.

I found Edith sitting in the ER waiting room, knitting.

"I didn't know you could knit," I said.

Edith looked up at me and, put her knitting down, stood, and hugged me to herself.

"Oh, Marra! You poor dear! What a day this has been for you. I'm sorry that we had to take Jayne away from you."

"That's okay, have you heard anything about H.B.?"

"He's having an angioplasty. They found a large blockage in his left ventricle, and they are putting stents in. They said he should be fine, but he'll have to be in the hospital for at least a week. How's Shelby?"

Edith was just as relieved as I had been upon hearing the news, but she was genuinely relaxed, whereas I was still keyed up. I shared with her how H.B. had asked me to tell her that he loved her, and she smiled sweetly.

"And I love him! I am so happy that he's come into my life, and that we have so much to share, including a grandson! Can you imagine my good fortune, Marra?"

Edith suggested that I try and reach Albert to give him the good news about Shelby. I called Albert's New York office, and was told that Mr. Williams was on vacation, and couldn't be reached until next week, so I asked to speak with his personal assistant.

"This is Pam, may I help you?" a friendly voice said.

"Yes, Pam, my name is Marra Dallas, I'm Mrs. Williams' sister, I'm wondering where Mr. Williams is."

"He is on vacation this week, I'm not sure exactly where," she lied. Every personal assistant knows exactly where her boss is at all times, in case of an emergency.

Now it was my turn to lie, "You see, Pam, that's a problem. My sister has had an emergency, and she is currently unconscious. I need to get in touch with my brother-in-law, as legally he is her next of kin."

She was quiet for a minute, no doubt thinking about what to do.

"Perhaps you could give me the number of Mr. Williams' lawyer, maybe he could help me," I suggested. That did it.

"Oh, wait a minute," she said, "I do have an emergency contact number here!"

When Albert answered the phone, he sounded like he'd just come up for air. "Hello?"

"Albert, it's Marra. Shelby's just had major surgery. Where the hell are you?" I demanded.

"What? What are you talking about? Where is she?" he questioned.

"No, I asked first. Where are you?"

"I, ah, I'm away for the week, on business."

"Oh, really? You're secretary said you were on vacation, and I'm wondering, why would my brother-in-law go on vacation when his wife is having major surgery?"

"What are you talking about, Marra? First of all, we've been separated for three months, and second of all, how am I supposed to know that something's happened to her if nobody called me?" he asked.

Why didn't she tell us they were separated? Why didn't she tell her kids about her illness? They probably didn't know about their parent's separation either. Why the hell does everything have to be a big secret with her? Doesn't she realize that the truth always comes out in the end anyway? Secrets only fester, and turn into a cancer, and spread their infection, invading into your life no matter how much you might try and deny them. Her physical illness was like a manifestation of her emotional illness.

When I hung up from speaking with Albert, who promised that he'd be out to see her the next day, I returned to the E.R. area, where Edith sat, still knitting away, and filled her in. Just then, a nurse in scrubs pushed through the double doors and shouted, "Maybank?"

Edith and I stood simultaneously, and the nurse motioned us forth, through the double doors, and into a glass-walled waiting room, where the surgeon stood, still in scrubs.

"I'm so sorry, Mrs. Maybank," he said, believing that Edith was H.B.'s wife, "It was a much more serious condition than we'd anticipated, and although we tried our very best, Mr. Maybank didn't survive the surgery."

Edith looked at me with a quizzical expression on her face, "I don't believe this, Marra, it's a lie!"

I looked up at the window, and saw H.B. and John Lloyd in an embrace, and I felt the familiar feeling of loss and love, simultaneously.

"No, Edith, he's telling you the truth, H.B.'s gone."

"How do you know that Marra?" she whispered.

"Because I see him standing beside John Lloyd, just there, by the window," I said, pointing toward the ghosts I could plainly see. Edith nodded, as if what I'd just said had made perfect sense to her, and looked toward the window, seeing nothing but the sky outside.

It was decided by Edith, Will, and Missy, that H.B's body would be cremated there in New Jersey, and the remains shipped back to Charleston, where he would be memorialized a month later.

Will flew up to be with Edith, Jayne, and the kids, and I stayed for an additional week before returning home. I made daily trips over to see them, but stayed with Shelby, and I was there when Albert came by to see her. I overheard a conversation between them, he kept asking her why she didn't tell him, and she kept saying, "Because it wouldn't have changed anything, Albert!"

It had taken me two days to convince Shelby to call the girls. Darcy came home at once, but I think that she was more upset about her parent's separation, than she was about her mother's brush with death. Deidre was in the middle of her summer semester class in Paris (France, not Texas), and at her mother's urging, stayed there. I heard Shelby on the phone with Deidre, assuring her that she was going to be perfectly fine, and that she wouldn't have called at all except that *Marra Dallas* kept hounding her about it.

The day before I left, I tried my best to have a heartfelt conversation with Shelby, and tell her how I had prayed that she'd survive, and we'd have the chance to spend more time together.

"Jesus, Marra, you're like a soap opera, you blow everything out of proportion. I only had minor surgery, and you're moping around here like my prognosis was fatal!" she scolded.

"Shelby, I'm mourning H.B., and sad for Edith and Will. Don't you ever stop to think that maybe everything isn't about you?" I yelled, surprising myself with the anger that had welled up inside of me so unexpectedly.

Shelby's eyes widened in horror, like I'd slapped her. In a way, I suppose it was like I had, I'd hardly ever stood up to her in my entire life. She wasn't used to my asserting myself when it came to dealing with her.

"You know, Marra, I don't know why I put up with you at all. Why don't you just go back to Jayne's, you're probably more comfortable there anyway!" She said, and her animosity toward me was evident by her demeanor.

I gathered my things and left quietly, and returned to Edith's house without sharing the little scene with anyone. They'd all had enough grief, and by comparison this was minor; but I found myself crying on the plane on the way home, not only for losing H.B., but for once again losing my sister. We'd never be able to share the sorrows and joys of our lives with each other the way in which sisters should. But that never was, and would never be; I couldn't get close to Shelby, no matter what I did, or said. I know that early on in our lives, it was just as much my fault as hers. I'd never opened up to anyone either. But as I grew up, I began to let those walls down. Maybe it was because I'd experienced love. When you allow yourself to love, and to be loved, you realize that it's worth the risk. As Alfred Lord Tennyson said, *'Tis better to have loved and lost, than never to have loved at all'*.

CHAPTER THIRTY-FOUR

The month between H.B.'s death and his memorial service gave us all time to digest the fact that he was gone. I hurt for myself, but felt much more pain for Edith, who had lost another love, and for Will, who had lost the father that he'd known for too short of a time. I knew that John Lloyd had been there to welcome his father to the other side, and that had brought me comfort, but I was reluctant to share that with anyone, lest they think that I'd lost my mind. Edith had easily accepted what I'd said at the hospital, but she'd been in shock upon hearing the news that H.B. had died.

I'd never told anyone that I could see and hear those who had passed on. It was one thing to admit that they had come to me in a dream, I'd heard lots of people say that they had dreamed of departed loved ones, but I'd never heard anyone say that they'd heard them speak to them, sing to them, or appear to them, while they were awake. As always, I was afraid of judgment and rejection.

We traveled together to Charleston to celebrate the man who had been the love of my mother's life, the father of my brother, as well as the father of my best friend, and the love of my other best friend's mother's life. It was incredible and amazing to me what an important role H.B. Maybank had played in my life, and how his life had snaked around my own, weaving in and out, in time and space. We gathered once again in that old Methodist church, the place where Annabelle had dreamed that John Lloyd and I would one day be married, the place where I sang to my sweet love that last time. Missy sat quietly now for the first time in her life, as we gathered to remember her father, as we had her mother, not so long ago. She held onto Will on one side, and to her husband on the other, as tears trickled silently down her cheeks. Maybe all of her histrionics had been for the benefit of her daddy all those years, and now that he was gone, there was no reason to perform anymore.

Before leaving Charleston, H.B.'s lawyer asked Will and I to join Missy for the reading of his last will and testament. I understood why he wanted Will there, but I didn't know why he'd invited me.

I was astonished, Will was pleased, and Missy was horrified, that H.B. Maybank had divided his entire fortune between the three of us. If not for explicit instructions that H.B. had left behind, there was no doubt in my mind that Missy would have contested the will. H.B.'s attorney read the letter of explanation that laid out his reasoning, so there was no doubt of what his wishes had been. H.B.'s letter made it clear that he'd always thought of me as a daughter, especially since I was a sister to his only remaining son, and that I would have been married to his other son, should he had survived. I'm sure that H.B. had known better than that, but it was his final word on the subject, and Missy had no room to protest. Will and I both agreed that we'd deed the Harleston Village Mansion to Missy, since it had been her childhood home.

Will was adamant about keeping the beach house on Sullivan's Island that he'd helped H.B. rebuild after the hurricane. It had been their favorite retreat, where they'd go to spend time as father and son. They'd lost so many years together, and H.B. was trying to make that up to Will. I can't imagine the guilt that H.B. must have carried for all of those years, knowing that he had a child out there that he didn't know. I was glad that Will had that beach house, with all of its special memories. He would bring his own son there over the years, and share the stories of his grandfather with him. I was happy to have anything at all, and truly felt like an interloper in the whole affair.

I thought that Missy was going to pass out, her face was beet red, and she was fanning herself a mile a minute. Her husband started to react when he saw her, and she placed her hand on his arm and said, "We'll call our own lawyer, and deal with them later!"

It wouldn't have taken much for me to give in, and sign everything over to her, but Will wouldn't hear of it. He said that it was what H.B. had wanted, and that they'd discussed it at length. H.B. had told Will that Missy had been handed everything in life, as had her silver-spoon husband, and that they'd do better in life without being handed any more. It made me feel a little less guilty about accepting H.B.'s money.

CHAPTER THIRTY~FIVE

Alex and John Dallas were delighted to have me back home, although between baseball, skateboarding, and my son's new surfing passion, I felt like I was invading the boy's club. I noticed some pink, folded-up paper in my son's room, and when I went to pick it up, he snatched it from my hand.

"Mama! That's personal, if you don't mind!"

"Sorry!"

I mussed his curls, and left him to his computer, music blasting in the background, and went outside to where Alex was working in the garden.

"I think our boy has a girlfriend!" I stated.

"Are ju keeding? He has like fī!"

"Five?"

"Sí, fī! Chelsee-a, Loo-ren, Jess-ē-ca, Crees-tina, y Kahlua."

"Okay, I got Chelsea, Lauren, Jessica and Christina, but are you sure that last one is Kahlua?"

"I don' know, someting like Kahlua."

"Chloe?"

"Sí, Kah-louie! Esta bien!"

I hadn't had a good belly laugh in a long time, and there was nothing like Alex's fractured English to make me chuckle. He always looked so pleased with himself when he'd make me laugh, and that was why he'd purposely exaggerate his accent. It went back to the day we met, me repeating everything he'd said. It wasn't that I couldn't understand him, it was just that I was so flustered looking at him - that tight shirt, those bulging biceps, not to mention those glutes!

There were times when we'd meet Spanish-speaking friends of his, that he'd give me a hard time. He'd introduce me as his English teacher, "Meeeses Doll-ass", forcing me to punch him in front of his friends. I could understand almost everything he'd say in Spanish, except for when he'd speed-talk. John Dallas could pretty much keep up with him, but that was because he'd been learning the language since he was fí.

Alex's English was much better than my Spanish, except when he'd lay on the heavy accent to try and trip me up, or to make me laugh. He was a funny guy, always finding humor in everything. When Alex's mother came from Puerto Rico for a visit, I saw where he had gotten his easy-going manner, and great sense of humor.

Rosíta Serrano de la Cruz was a small, pretty woman, with dark eyes, and auburn hair. She hugged me like she'd known me all of her life, and fawned over John Dallas, only she called him 'Juán Dull-ees'; and he was enamored with her.

She showed him how to read tea leaves, something I remembered my paternal grandmother doing when I was small; and she told him how the lines in his palm indicated fame and fortune.

"Sí," Alex said to me, "That's what she 'tol me when I was a boy. Mamá, she lie."

"Alejandro!" Rosíta yelled, "Cállate!"

"Sí Mamí, Lo siento."

Everything they said to one another was with a smile or a wink, never in anger. She had the same pleasant disposition that Alex had, and it was a joy spending time with her. The week flew by, and I was sorry that our visit was coming to an end. I promised her that we all would come to Puerto Rico to visit with her soon, and apologized that I hadn't met her sooner.

On the day before she was scheduled to leave, Rosíta asked Alex and I to come out into the backyard, saying she needed to speak with us privately. She was sitting on Papa Joe's old, white wicker rocker, and motioned for us to sit across from her, on the settee. The sun was shining shafts of light through the palms, hibiscus and bougainvillea, giving Rosíta an ethereal glow.

"Is no my busy-ness, pero I muss to tell you, Marrá, y tú, Alejandro. Why ju' no marry?"

Alex and I looked at each other, and we both burst out laughing.

"Is no funny!" Rosíta yelled. "Dees' es muy importante! Ju' have a young boy to theenk of. He needs padres, dos padres." She looked at Alex with a very sad expression, and said, "Alejandro, I no raise ju' to live like dees', ju' mus' to marry!"

"Sí Mamí," he said, and then stood up in front of me, dropped down on one knee, and said, "Te amo con todo, mi corazón. Will you marry me, Marra Dallas?"

I didn't know if he was serious, or just performing this little number to make his mother happy, knowing that she wouldn't know whether we'd gotten married or not, once she returned to Puerto Rico. He hadn't used his heavily accented English, like he did when he was playing with me, which indicated sincerity. I searched his face, looking for a wink or smirk; there was nothing. His eyes were wide and clear, and when he realized that I had been hesitating because I didn't know if he was serious, he leaned in close and whispered in my ear.

"I love you, Marra, with all my heart, please, say jes' to me?"

He searched my eyes with his, and I said, "Jes!"

Alex lifted me up into the air, and laughed out loud. Rosíta squealed with delight, which brought John Dallas running outside to see what the commotion was all about.

"What's going on, guys? What happened?"

"Oh, Juán Dull-ees! Is good news! Ju' Mamí y Alejandro, they get marry!" Rosíta exclaimed, as she grabbed onto him, and danced him around the courtyard.

We had to postpone Rosíta's departure, because she insisted that we had to celebrate our engagement, and boy did we ever! Rosíta threw a party the likes of which my family had never seen. She cooked for two days, and with the aid of John Dallas and Alex, she had every inch of my house, inside and out, beautifully decorated with colorful flowers, and white, satin ribbons. There were white lanterns hanging all around the garden, and bouquets of flowers in decorative pots everywhere. It looked like something out of a Martha Stewart magazine.

Will, Jayne, and their two kids came, as did all of our friends, as well as John Dallas's friends. The food was magnificent; roast pork, fried plantains, bacalaitos (crunchy cod fritters), empanadillas (crescent-shaped turnovers filled with crab and lobster), chicken and rice, and an assortment of flaky, fruit-filled pastries. Alex made sangria, mojítos, and piña coladas, and when night fell, he lit the chiminea (the outdoor fireplace).

Just when I thought it couldn't get any better, Alex presented me with the most gorgeous, platinum, 2-carat, aquamarine and diamond ring - princess cut, naturally. I'm not a jewelry person, but this ring was the most beautiful thing I'd ever seen. I couldn't have picked out anything better myself. Alex gently brushed the tears from my eyes, as I admired the lovely token of his love.

I remember sitting outside alone after everyone had gone, and Alex and Rosíta were inside cleaning up the kitchen. I was looking up into the sky at the twinkling stars, and crescent moon, that was hanging low over the gulf, and I felt like all was right with the world. It took me forty-five years to get here, but it was all good - finally. I knew that I'd still have hard times, and heartbreak, but for right now, I had perfect peace, and I was loving life.

Six months later, Alex and I flew to Puerto Rico to be married, with John Dallas in tow. Because Alex had insisted that he was going to take care of all of the planning, I had absolutely no idea what I was getting myself into. I don't know what I was expecting, but I was amazed by the entire affair.

Foolishly, I had imagined us traveling to a small town, riding on the backs of donkeys up a steep mountain trail, to a simple village, where Rosíta would be waiting with a few hundred of their closest relatives, none of whom spoke English. I imagined small, brown children throwing flower petals at us as we walked barefoot to an historic chapel, that was nestled in the side of a cliff. I don't know where I got these ideas from, but I was glad that I hadn't shared these thoughts with anyone, because I would have died of embarrassment.

Imagine my surprise when the limo that picked us up at the airport pulled up to the El Conquistador Resort. It was an amazing hotel that was perched atop a 300-foot cliff on Puerto Rico's northeast coast, overlooking the convergence of the Atlantic Ocean and the Caribbean Sea. The resort boasted a casino, spa, golf course, several silver spoon restaurants, and John Dallas's favorite, a water park!

Our suite was about eighteen hundred square feet, with two bedrooms, a living room, balconies, a kitchenette, stereo, plasma TV, and a computer. It was filled with tropical flowers, an amazing fruit platter, and a large bottle of champagne, that was chilling in a sterling silver ice bucket. For one week I was pampered, massaged, and fed, until I thought I would burst.

We were married ocean-side, with a small group of Alex's family in attendance, all of whom were fluent in English. It was heaven, perfect down to the smallest detail. I wore a simple, white cotton dress, and wore a crown of small, white flowers in my hair that Rosíta had fashioned for me. Alex wore a light beige cotton suit, with a gauzy white shirt, and we were both barefoot. The priest who married us was a family friend, and kept the ceremony short and sweet. John Dallas was Alex's best man, and Alex's cousin Dolly was my maid of honor, even though we'd only been acquainted for about three hours at that point.

Rosíta cried throughout the entire ceremony, and afterward, to lighten the mood, Alex's brother Carlos yelled, "Mamí, I 'tol ju' he was not gay!" We all laughed, as Rosíta chased him around the dining room, hitting him over the head with the bouquet. Besides the birth of my son, it was the highlight of my life.

CHAPTER THIRTY-SIX

By the spring of 2001, my sister was barely holding on to life by a thread. I visited as often as possible, because I knew that soon there'd be no point in returning. Only after I'd threatened to call her doctor, Shelby admitted to me that she'd known her true diagnosis before her surgery, and had instructed her doctor to tell all of us that she was going to be fine. She insisted that it was her decision, and hers alone, and that she'd done all of us a favor – after all, if we'd known her dire circumstances, we'd have driven her insane with our worrying, and there's no point in worrying when there's nothing one can do to change things.

It was typical Shelby, she always had to be in control, even of other people's emotions. God forbid we tried to get close to her, knowing that her time was short! Once again, Shelby would dictate her relationships, what other people wanted, or how they felt, wasn't anything she'd reflect upon.

Deidre was graduating from the University of Texas in May, and the entire family (with the exception of Shelby, because she was too weak) was in attendance. Though we tried to keep it upbeat for Deidre's sake, there was an air of mournfulness over the day. I kept thinking that Shelby should have been here, she would have taken control over everyone, and everything. We wouldn't have had to think about anything, because Shelby would have had it all figured out.

Albert had put us all up at the Driskill Hotel, a Romanesque masterpiece of architecture that had been built in 1886. He wined and dined us, as he regaled us with a fascinating account of the hotel's history, and he was charming and accommodating. I'd never spent much time around Albert over the years, and was surprised to find that he was actually a very nice man. He was very friendly to Alex, and took great interest in John Dallas, introducing him to everyone as *'my nephew'*. Albert spent quite a lot of time talking to my son, asking him about his life, and his interests. He even offered to take Alex and John Dallas to a Yankee game the next time they came north, and promised to introduce them to many of the team members. We found out through that conversation that Albert was a close friend of George Steinbrenner. On the surface, we looked like one big, happy family; Albert with his two beautiful, adult daughters, Will and Jayne with Bridget and Barrett, and Alex and me with John Dallas.

We all managed to enjoy the graduation, but I kept thinking that Shelby should be there. It made me so sad to think that this family would go on without her, even though she had never seemed to take much joy from any of us. She was still a part of us, she'd always been, and she always would be.

By the first of June, Shelby was bedridden, and Will and I flew up to be by her side until the end. Deidre was staying home for the summer so that she could be there for Shelby, and Darcy had transferred to the New York office. It was less than an hour's commute from 26 Federal Plaza to her mother's home in Caldwell. As hard as it was for the girls to see their mother in that condition, they were a great comfort to Shelby, she could pretend that everything was fine.

When I went into my sister's darkened room, I was stunned to see how beautiful she still looked, and so close to the end of her life. Even though she was looking right at me, I wasn't sure if she realized I was there. I thought perhaps she couldn't see me clearly.

"Shelby, it's me, Marra. I'm here, honey."

"I know it's you, Marra, I'm looking right at you."
Even near death she was condescending, but rather than
finding it offensive or hurtful, I found it humorous. "I can
see you," she sighed, and then closed her eyes. "Marra,"
she said, with her eyes still closed, "sing that song to me
that you used to sing to me when we were little."

"What song is that, Shelby?"

"You know, the one that you used to sing when
we'd walk to the store for Mama. The one you used to sing
so that I'd shut up, and stop complaining - that Beatles'
song, that one you'd sing that you loved me more."

"Oh, I know which one," I said, and I sang *In My
Life*, which really was an appropriate song for my life.
What Shelby really wanted to hear was at the end of the
song, *"I loved you more"*; and so I sang it to her, over and
over, for the next ten days, and I was singing it to her
when she drew her last breath. I went on singing it, as I
saw her spirit rise up out of her body, and I saw John
Lloyd take her by the hand to usher her to the place where
he lived while he was away from me. Shelby stopped, and
turned to look in my direction, and she smiled. It was a
warm, loving smile, that I felt deep within my heart and
soul, and I realized, in that moment, that she'd always
loved me, just as I had always loved her, and always
would.

CHAPTER THIRTY-SEVEN

I stood behind my niece's chair under the funeral canopy, on the same plot of land where my mother was buried. It had been one of Shelby's last wishes, to be buried with Mama. Unlike the day of Mama's funeral, this day was sunny and warm, with big, puffy, white clouds, floating in a cerulean sky. Deidre sat in front of me and sobbed, shoulders heaving, head down, while Darcy stood stoically next to me. They were a contrast in every way, dark and light; they reminded me of Shelby and me in some ways.

John Dallas was next to me, and Alex next to him. Will, Jayne, Bridget, Barrett, and Edith were behind us.

Albert was on the other side of Darcy, and he, too, was sobbing. On the day that Shelby died, he wailed as though he'd lost the love of his life, though I'd never seen them kiss, or hold hands, or demonstrate affection for each other in any way. Perhaps she had been the love of his life, but he most certainly wasn't the love of hers. Shelby had always spoken *of* him as a 'good provider' and *to* him as though he was her servant. Although they had been separated for a period of time, Albert had insisted on moving back into the house when he realized that Shelby was ill, even though she'd protested. Shelby only called his name when she needed him to fetch something for her, and seemed to prefer that he stay out of her room. I found myself feeling sorry for him, because he clearly adored her, while she merely tolerated him.

As the minister droned on, I watched the clouds float by, and suddenly heard John Lloyd singing *In My Life*, somewhere behind me. I turned to my right, and looked over my shoulder, and saw him standing next to a man. They were about forty yards away from our group of mourners. John Lloyd smiled at me, and motioned with his hand, beckoning me over toward them.

When the graveside service was finished, and the mourners dispersed toward the limousines, I whispered to Alex that I'd be right back, and I headed toward the man who still stood in the same spot, although John Lloyd had disappeared. As I approached the man, he looked down, as though he was looking at someone's headstone plaque on the ground next to him.

"Hello," I said, "I'm Shelby's sister, Marra."

He looked up at me quizzically, eyebrows raised. I could see that he'd been crying. "How did you know? Did she tell you about me?" he asked.

"Sort of," I lied.

He extended his hand to me, "Daniel Ryan."

"Marra Dallas," I said, as I took his hand.

"Oh, I know who you are," he said, "Shelby spoke of you often."

"How long were you and Shelby . . . friends?"
"Twenty-five years next month," he said, with great sadness.

"Twenty-five years? You have known my sister for the past twenty-five years?" I asked incredulously.

He smiled, and reached into his jacket pocket, and brought out a card. He handed it to me, saying, "You'd better get going, they're looking for you," and his eyes looked toward the road.

I turned, and I saw Alex standing alongside the limo we'd come in, and he motioned to his wrist, as in 'time'. I took the business card from Daniel's outstretched hand.

"Call me," he said, "Maybe we can get together sometime and talk."

"Okay," I said, "I *will* call you," and then I turned, and started walking away from him. I stopped abruptly, turned back toward him, and asked, "Would you like to join us?"

"I don't think I'd better. Maybe another time you and I can visit," he said sadly.

I walked back toward the limo in a daze. I looked up at the clouds, and saw Shelby's smiling face.

Alex saw the look on my face and asked, "Are ju' okay, Princess?"

I hugged him tightly, and sobbed into his shoulder. What secrets had Shelby kept for all of these years? What had prevented her from sharing her life with me? I knew now, based on the revelation I'd received at the moment of her passing, that she'd always loved me, so why couldn't she trust me?

Albert held the funeral repast at Green Brook, his golf and country club. It was a lovely venue for the several hundred people in attendance, most of them there to schmooze, judging by the festive atmosphere. A string quartet playing Vivaldi performed on a raised platform, next to an ice sculpture of a larger-than-life angel, an assortment of the finest foods chilling at its base.

Tuxedoed servers carried shining silver trays of champagne, and something pink in Martini glasses, which I assumed was something that Shelby had favored. I could hear dozens of conversations, and people laughing, and exclaiming, *"I haven't seen you in ages, darling! How in the world are you?"*

Shelby would have loved this, mostly because she would have been the center of attention. Shelby could work a crowd like nobody's business, with her blonde tresses piled fashionably into a chignon, her large, hazel cat-eyes, batting their fake, two-inch lashes, and her perfect white teeth, flashing behind a seductively pouty smile. Men were enamored with her, and women genuinely admired her, at the very least her beauty, elegance and style. None of them knew the real Shelby, even I didn't know the real Shelby, if, in fact, there was a 'real' Shelby. These people lived in the superficial world of material possessions, and appearances, and were taken by shiny things, and charming personalities – and Shelby was certainly shiny and charming. That same charm and charisma that she'd had as a child was in abundance whenever she was out in public; it was always as if the sun shone down directly over her head every day, just as the little black cloud would always seem to hover just above my own. I couldn't believe that she was gone, and that these strangers were the people who were left to mourn her. And what of Daniel Ryan, Shelby's mystery man of the past twenty-five years? How could she have kept a secret like that? Snap out of it, I thought, we're talking the Queen of Secrets here, just like her mother before her.

Just as I started to stand, to announce that I'd officially had enough of this ridiculous affair, I heard a somewhat familiar woman's voice calling my name. I turned toward the voice, and saw an older version of Brady, standing near the entrance, head searching the crowd for me. Our eyes met, mouths broadened with our grins, and we hurried toward each other across the room.

"Marra Dallas!" she yelled.

"Brady Dallas!" I yelled back.

We embraced, then pulled back to search each other's faces, and embraced again.

"I saw the obituary, I'm so sorry Marra. I would have come sooner, but I couldn't get a flight."

Needless to say, Brady and I found a quiet place to talk, and catch up with the abridged versions of each another's lives. Brady and husband number three were living in Las Vegas. Her two daughters from her first marriage lived near her, one was single, and the other was married, with four little girls. Brady knew about Shelby's death, because her husband was an entertainment lawyer who subscribed to the New York Times. While flipping through it out of shear boredom, she happened upon an article about the death of Shelby Williams, wife of the president of Firestone Tire. It was the name *Shelby* that had caught her eye, and as she read on, she saw that Mrs. Williams was survived by her sister, Marra Dallas of Florida. Brady knew that I'd be here, and grabbed the first flight out of Vegas to find me.

Brady looked the same, but better. She was older, and that had been the first thing that I'd noticed about her, but the more my eyes searched her face, I saw something other than fine lines. I saw the beauty that comes with the knowledge of oneself. Brady was a pretty girl, who had matured into a beautiful woman. We talked for what seemed like a very short time, but in reality had been hours. I introduced her to everyone, and invited her to come back to Edith's with us so that we could continue our reunion, but she had to turn around and catch a late flight back to Vegas because she had a meeting in the morning with the Governor. Brady, it turned out, was the director of the drug and alcohol rehabilitation program for the state of Nevada. We exchanged information, and promised to keep in touch on a regular basis from that moment forward.

As I hugged her goodbye, I was overwhelmed with gratitude that she'd come all this way for just a few hours, in order to reconnect with me. I felt so much love *from* her, and *for* her. It was as if I'd found a lost sister, just after losing a sister. A sister found, for a sister lost. Now I understood how H.B. must have felt meeting Will after burying John Lloyd, what a mix of emotions! I understood how, although your heart is breaking for the one you've lost, your heart sings at the chance to love someone else.

As I stood out on Edith's patio that night in the darkness, I was listening to the babbling brook below, and thinking of Shelby. Looking up, I glimpsed the brightest of stars streaking across the sky, just over my head. I knew that it was Shelby's final mark on this world. I waved my hand, and said, "Goodbye, my beautiful sister!"

I felt a peace that I hadn't felt in a long time. I was suddenly filled with a knowing, that everything was alright, everything in the universe was just as it should be. That night, when I lay my head upon my pillow, I drifted into the soundest sleep.

CHAPTER THIRTY-EIGHT

I phoned Daniel Ryan the next day, and we met the day after that, at the same restaurant where Edith and I had met Shelby and Darcy that first time, after my release from juvenile detention. We sat in silence as he studied my face, searching, I'm sure, for some resemblance to my sister.

"I don't see it," he finally said.

"We don't look alike at all, I look like my mother, and Shelby favored my father's side."

"But you have the same voice," he said, "you sound just like her."

"You think so?" I asked. It wasn't the first time I'd heard that.

Daniel smiled at me, and then looked down, and fiddled with his menu. I didn't know how long I could stand the mystery, so I forged ahead.

"So tell me, Mr. Ryan, what exactly was the nature of your relationship with my sister?"

He looked at me earnestly, then announced, "She was the love of my life, and the mother of my only child."

His words hit me like a ton of bricks. Not that she was the love of his life, I could easily imagine that there were many men who'd fallen in love with Shelby over the years – but the fact that he'd said that Shelby was the mother of his only child. I calculated quickly, he'd said that they'd known each other for 25 years, so that left Darcy out. He was talking about Deidre, and as I searched his face, I could see it clearly; the dark eyes, the shape of his face, the full lips, even the way his teeth were spaced.

"She never told me, not that that's a big surprise. Shelby never shared much about her life with me." I could hear a touch of anger in my own voice, causing me to think that I sounded like Shelby more than ever.

"She wanted to tell you," he said, "she'd planned on telling you, after you became a mother yourself. But then your husband cheated on you, and you divorced him so quickly, she knew that you'd never understand, and so she decided she'd better not."

"I'm sorry Mr. Ryan . . ." I began.

"Dan, please call me Dan."

"I'm sorry Dan, but I don't buy that. Shelby never shared anything personal with me. She may have given you that excuse as the reason why she didn't share with me that you were Deidre's father, but that's just not true."

"Listen Marra, I understand that this is upsetting for you. I thought long and hard about telling you at all, but when you came over to me at the funeral, I thought perhaps you suspected. Shelby told me that you'd commented on Deidre's eyes being so dark, and knowing how smart you are, she was sure that you'd figured it out."

I flashed back to that conversation, and Shelby's anger over my innocent comment. Suddenly, pieces of a rather intricate puzzle were beginning to fit into place.

He continued, "I know that Shelby wasn't a warm, fuzzy personality. She had that wall around her that looked, for all intent and purpose, that she was unfeeling and cold; but nothing could be further from the truth. Your sister was a kind, and loving woman, whose feelings ran deep; but she kept that wall up in order to protect herself, not to hurt others. I can't tell you how often she spoke of you, and how proud she was of you, and how far you'd come. Not long ago, she finally told me the story of your mother's death, and how you'd tried to defend her, and what it had cost you. She said that you were the finest, bravest person she'd ever known, and that she'd kept her secrets from you because she thought you'd be disappointed in her."

"*Me*, disappointed in *her*? I'd always thought that she disapproved of me. And as far as my being brave, why, then, did she tell me she was embarrassed of me?"

Dan looked shocked at that, then replied, "I never heard that from her Marra, I only heard good things where you were concerned."

I stopped to consider it all; it just didn't jibe with the Shelby I knew, but then, did I ever really know Shelby at all? Apparently not! All of this information was a lot to take in, and although I had new information, I had more questions than answers.

"Do the girls know about you?"

"Both girls have met me over the years, but only as a friend of the family, and their mother's financial advisor. I think that it's possible that Darcy has some idea, because since she's become an agent, she's treated me differently, as though I'm a suspect."

"Does Albert know?"

"As far as I know, he doesn't. I've been introduced to him as Shelby's financial advisor, which, by the way, I am. Shelby allowed me to come to the house more often once they were separated, but by that time, she knew she was ill, and thought there'd be no point in upsetting everyone."

I rolled my eyes and shook my head at that, and he laughed.

"I know," he said, "typical Shelby, right?"

"Right! She sure had some web of lies going! I have to give her credit for her secrecy. She's her mother's daughter, that's for sure. Did you know that my mother kept my brother's true paternity a secret?"

"Yes, Shelby told me about it when it all came out. Even though I'm sure she kept things from me, she probably confided in me more than anyone else. Tell me, Marra, will you tell anyone what I've told you today?"

"I'll tell my husband, but as far as Deidre goes, don't you think that's up to you, Mr. Ryan?"

He looked perplexed. I'm not sure if it was because I'd gone back to calling him 'Mr. Ryan', or because he wasn't sure how to answer me. I don't know what he'd expected of our meeting today, or what he thought I'd do about the bombshell he'd dropped on me.

"Honestly Marra, I'm not sure what to do now. I'd like nothing better than to tell Deidre, otherwise, how am I ever going to see her? But I'm afraid of what this revelation will do to all of them; the girls and their . . . I mean Albert."

"Well, if you want my two cents, here it is - my mother went to her grave with her secrets, just like my sister did, but we all found out in the end, though. The saddest thing is that my brother had never had the benefit of knowing his only brother, and his time with his biological father was much too short. We change the course of people's lives when we keep secrets from them, and lie to them. I'm going to leave it to you, Mr. Ryan. You do whatever you think is the right thing to do, she is *your* daughter. But just think about what will happen if you wait, and she ends up finding out some other way, how do you think that will affect your relationship with her?"

I gathered my things and rose to leave.

"I'm sorry if I offended you, Marra," he said, as he extended a hand to me.

I took his hand and said, "You haven't offended me, Dan, I just need some time to digest all of this. I had no idea that Shelby was capable of keeping a secret like that, but I suppose I shouldn't be surprised. I've always said that she was her mother's daughter. I hope that you'll come to a good conclusion."

As I drove back to Edith's house, I thought about all I'd learned this day, and tried to absorb it all. Almost everything I thought I knew about my sister was either wrong, or off base. All of my life, I'd fruitlessly chased a relationship with a woman that I'd hardly known, and believed that it was because she didn't want to connect with me. Now, I wasn't so sure. Was she only guarding her secrets? Was she afraid that I wouldn't keep them for her?

EPILOGUE

2001, Age 47

Sunset

September 11, 2001, was yet another day that will live in infamy. Surely, I couldn't have been the only person who had witnessed all of those departed souls, rising up from the burning towers, and floating toward the Heavens. Surely, there are others like me, who see the spirits of the departed.

John Lloyd had appeared to me early that morning, singing a mournful rendition of *Bridge Over Troubled Water*, and I knew for sure that a dark storm was approaching. If he'd found it necessary to warn me of imminent darkness and heartache in advance, I believed that it was his way of telling me, that whatever terrible thing was coming, it was inevitable. Still I, like everyone else, sat in shocked terror, as I witnessed the horrifying events of that day.

Although I knew that every soul who left this world was headed to a better place, I mourned for all of those who loved them, the ones who would be left behind, feeling like a piece of themselves had been cut off, and lost forever. I knew better, and yet, I mourned those I'd lost myself – and *I* could still see them occasionally. How horrible must it be for those who don't know, for those who believe that life on earth is all there is. Sometimes, I wish I could tell them, but I know they'd never believe me. They'd think I was crazy, or making it all up, in order to comfort them. Perhaps everyone needs to know their own truth, in their own time.

The events of that fateful day changed us all, and pushed some people to do things that they otherwise might not have done. They say that there were a record number of marriage licenses applied for after 9/11, a record number of babies born the following year, and a record number of people changing jobs, residences, and lifestyles. I realized that it was time for me to do the same, to open myself up in a way I'd always been too frightened to do. It was time for me to come clean about who I am.

I sat down with Alex and John Dallas, and finally told them my whole story, ghosts included. They'd both taken it much better than I'd expected, and I was more than a little surprised when my son admitted that he had seen Ellie, and H.B., after they'd passed. I felt great relief in telling the truth, so that my son would never have to feel like he had to hide *his* truth. Alex hadn't thought that either of us was crazy, because, as it turned out, his mother had always spoken of seeing departed souls. I felt a huge burden lift from my chest, and experienced a freedom I'd never had before. It was a cleansing for us all.

Daniel Ryan invited Deidre out to lunch the week following 9/11, and told her the whole truth, for better or worse. She took it quite well, saying that she'd always felt as though she didn't fit into her own family. Deidre then broke the news to Albert, who vowed to always take care of her, and be her father, regardless of biology; and when Deidre shared her news with Darcy, she knew at once that her sister had known all along. Darcy had simply asked her, *"How do you feel about that?"*

I understood how Deidre must have felt, finding out that the people in her family, the people who were closest to her, had lied, and kept secrets. I understood how she must have felt about her mother, going to her grave with her secrets, and never being able to question, or confront her. I hoped that she wouldn't waste too much time trying to figure it all out, because in the end, it really doesn't matter. People make the choices they make based upon a set of factors that may, or may not be correct. Some make their choices selfishly, and some make them altruistically. Some people live bravely, and let the truth define them, while others hide behind their secrets and lies, and tell themselves it's for a good cause, or a higher purpose. We can adjust the truth to fit our fabricated outline, or we can create our outline from the truth we've lived.

These things I know are true: My mother loved me, and I've never been sorry for taking the life of the man who murdered her. I only wish that she would have been brave enough in life to admit when she was wrong, and maybe she could have changed things for all of us. My sister loved me, the only way that she knew how to love, behind a wall that kept others at bay. I only wish that she would have known that she could have trusted me to be her friend while she was here. Maybe she would have made different choices, had she opened herself up, and shared with someone. John Lloyd had truly loved me, even after he left this world. I only wish that he could have been able to be who he really was while he was here, and didn't believe that he had to live a lie, in order to keep other people happy.

Secrets keep us from living truly, and lies prevent us from openly loving one another, and why? Who will judge us more harshly than we judge ourselves? What a burden to carry, and what a prison we create for ourselves - a prison of secrets and lies, that locks us away from those who are waiting to love us, just as we are.

I sit in the garden, savoring the bouquet of jasmine, and delighting in the dazzling profusion of color from the flowering bougainvillea. I am so grateful for the love of a wonderful husband, exceptional son, and a faithful dog. As the setting sun gleams its crimson tentacles into a violet sky, I am filled with peace and comfort, as I hear John Lloyd's lovely voice singing *Bridge Over Troubled Water*, urging me to sail on, and to shine . . .

28828335R00165

Made in the USA
Charleston, SC
23 April 2014